"HE'S SHOOTING AT YOU!" TULLY SHOUTED.

He grabbed Alec's arm and whirled him around. They both ran for cover as a third searching shot smashed into an empty storage drum behind the mess tent.

"Is that guy crazy?" Alec asked wrathfully. "What the hell is he doing?" As if in answer the distant rifleman shot again. Both Tully and Alec, lying flat on the dirt, waited, looking at each other with a wild bitterness in their eyes.

For twenty minutes they lay in the dirt while all the mining equipment was thoroughly worked over. Then, as abruptly as the shooting began, it now ended, and Tully rose and dashed for the mess tent. The cook had taken to the timber, but his rifle stood in the corner of the tent. Tully grasped it and lunged outside. He heard Alec running behind him. "I'm going to hunt that guy down and kill him," Tully said thinly. "Let's go!"

SILVER ROCK

LUKE SHORT

A DELL BOOK

Published by
Dell Publishing
a division of
Bantam Doubleday Dell Publishing Group, Inc.
666 Fifth Avenue
New York, New York 10103

ISBN: 0-440-20556-5

Reprinted by arrangement with the author's estate

Printed in the United States of America

Published simultaneously in Canada

March 1990

10 9 8 7 6 5 4 3 2 1

KRI

1

If they'd ever had a schedule for this narrow-gauge train, they'd lost it, Tully thought. He was due in at nine; it was eleven P.M. now, so that when he stepped out on the platform alongside the sleepy brakeman, the only other passenger, he couldn't see much of the town, Azurite. Even on this moonless night, though, the vaulting mountains on all sides of him blotted out the horizon stars, and there was a bite in the October air.

"Take it easy, soldier. So long," the brakeman said.

"Mister," Tully said.

The brakeman laughed. "Okay, Lieutenant. So long."

Tully picked up his flight bag and walked down the platform past the lighted bay window of the station. A pickup truck was backing up to the open door of the baggage car and the agent was waiting to help a couple of the train crew unload sacks of mail.

Suddenly it came, just as unpredictably as always. Tully dropped his bag and then, closer to falling than sitting, he eased himself down on the bag. There was no pain, just a total, rubbery numbness in both legs, which would soon pass. *I've been sitting down too long,* Tully thought. *He said it would do it.* He sat there a moment, a loose-jointed tall young man in worn flannels and sports jacket. He saw the covert stares of the train crew, and he glared back fiercely, knowing that in the dark his expression of anger was wasted. Presently, as if somebody had flicked an invisible switch, the feeling returned to his legs. He stretched them gingerly, then rose and picked up his bag.

One of the men in the bed of the truck called to him, "Stick around a minute and I'll give you a lift."

Tully said, "Thanks," and went around the front of the pickup, opened the door and climbed in past the wheel.

Tully's anger was gone. He said, "You're the taxi service, too."

"Yeah, and what would the government say to that?"

"Is the train always this late?"

"Only when they don't have trouble," the man said. He glanced down at the bag and by the light of the dash read aloud, "Lieutenant Tully B. Gibbs, U.S.M.C.," and recited the serial number.

Here it comes, Tully thought. *All the questions.*

The man only said, "What's the B. for?" and Tully said, "Bryan," and that was all. They drove a couple of blocks past unlighted buildings, and swung into the main street, turning right. Maybe three stores had their nightlights on. It was a wide, old-fashioned street, the buildings lining it mostly two-story and brick, a good half of them empty. A lone car, oddly enough a convertible with top down, was parked downstreet. The driver made a U-turn and pulled up in front of the hotel, Tully got out and thanked him, and the driver said, "I'll see you around," and drove off. Tully felt as alone as if he were standing in the middle of a big field.

The hotel was on the main four corners, a big three-story affair of brick with the tiled, pillared lobby of the typical mining boom-town hotel of the eighties. The clerk was an elderly man, and Tully disturbed his reading as he faced the desk and registered.

Tully asked then, "Ever fill this place up?"

"Not since 1905," the clerk said. Tully waited for him to tell the occasion, but he didn't.

"Can I get something to eat this late?"

"Two doors down," the clerk said, pointing.

The restaurant was a converted barroom, with the old mahogany bar serving as counter. The waiter, who was also the cook, fried up an egg sandwich and opened two bottles of beer, one for Tully and one for himself. After serving Tully, he took his bottle and walked ten feet down the counter and leaned against the ornate mahogany back bar with its heavy plate-glass mirror.

He wanted to talk, Tully knew, so he said, "Not much business."

"There'll be a few Elks in around midnight, when they close up, but it's a pretty dead dump."

"Any mines working?"

"One. There's a few leasers, too, but it's mostly peanuts."

Go ahead and ask, Tully thought, and he said, "You wouldn't know Kevin Russel, would you?"

The waiter grinned. "The old man? Sure. He still walks down to the post office every day, but it takes some doing lately." Then: "You know Kevin?"

"His son."

The waiter shook his head. "Not anymore, you don't. Jimmy was killed in Korea."

"I know. I was with him."

"You don't say." The waiter came up to him then and set his bottle on the counter, his pale face sharp with interest. "Is it true the way they said he died?"

"In hospital?"

"No. Shot down and captured and no medical attention."

"He got the same attention we all got, and that was none."

"You were shot down too?"

"Jimmy was my radarman."

"You don't say," the cook said. "How'd you get back?"

"Our guys overran us. We were too crippled to move, so the Reds gave us water and left us for our guys to find."

"You don't say," the cook repeated. "Say, you ought to see old Kevin before you go. He'd like to see you."

"That's why I'm here," Tully said.

They talked some more about what a lousy war it was, then Tully paid his bill, said good night, stepped into the deserted street and turned toward the hotel. The red Ford convertible with the top down that he'd seen upstreet was coasting slowly across the four corners coming toward him. He could see a shock of long blond hair behind the wheel as the car passed under the street lamp. Tully was abreast of the hotel when the car came to a stop beside him.

A girl called, "Can you give me a hand?"

Tully stopped and looked and saw there was a man with the girl. She was driving; the man was staring at Tully, and now he said slowly, "Beat it, bud."

Tully stood still a moment, and when nobody spoke he moved out to the curb, stepped off it and came up to the car. He looked at the man, and even from there he could smell the barbershop on him. His black hair was slicked down and his sports shirt was open under his loud checked jacket. He was big, young, with a boxcar build.

A sport, Tully thought, and glanced at the girl. She didn't go with the big character beside her. She was pretty in a kind of worried way, but she looked as if, when everything that was out of hand was in again, she could smile easily. She wore a red sports coat with the biggest plaid Tully had ever seen, a white silk scarf, gray gloves, and she might have been twenty-four.

Tully said, "What's the trouble?"

"I've been trying to dump him for an hour. He won't go."

Tully didn't look at the man, he looked at her. "Why won't he?"

"He's drunk."

Tully looked at the man now. "True or false, chum?"

"Half true," the man said. "My car, though."

"Is he your date?" Tully asked the girl.

"Yes."

Tully stepped back and said, "Well, have fun," and turned and went into the hotel. As the door closed behind him, he heard the clashing of gears as the convertible shot away from the hotel.

Picking up his key and bag, Tully went up to his room, a front one. Opening his bag, he changed into pajamas and then started unpacking. Midway through the chore, he thought he heard a car pass and went over to the window and looked out. It was the red convertible again, headed the other way.

If she wants out, why doesn't she drive home? he thought sourly.

He finished unpacking, and then threw his bag in the back of the closet. *Not too far back,* he thought, *you may be packing again tomorrow.*

Turning out the light, he walked to the window and looked out. The town was dark, except for an occasional light, and utterly soundless; beyond it the mountains loomed lonely and black. *This is the place,* he thought. *This is the stake. It's got to be.*

Next morning at a little after nine Tully, following the clerk's directions, stepped out into the chill sunlight, crossed the unpaved street and headed for the railroad tracks, bound for Kevin Russel's shack down on the river flats.

In the bright day, Azurite had an air of engaging raffishness. It was undeniably untidy: its brick was weathered and sloughing, its boards were a rich brown with age, new paint was a rarity, and its cracked sidewalks of ancient concrete were buckled with the frost of seventy mountain winters. Tully liked it all.

The street petered out at the tracks, and he took a weed-bordered path down through a tangle of chokecherry bushes to the river bottom, where he picked up a dirt road and followed it a hundred yards to a sagging picket fence around a tiny lot. Here, lying in the deep shade of massive cottonwoods, was a small unpainted house.

The gate was off, and Tully took the short stretch of rotting boardwalk to the porch. His knock on the screen door brought a stirring inside the house, and presently a small old man, straight-backed and slow-moving, appeared at the door.

"You're Mr. Russel, Jimmy's father," Tully said. "I'm Tully Gibbs."

The old man might have been slow-moving, but there was

nothing slow about his thought processes, Tully observed. Immediately, he opened the screen door and stuck out his hand.

"Lieutenant Gibbs, Jimmy's friend," old Kevin said softly. "I *am* glad to see you." He looked searchingly at Tully with the palest blue eyes Tully had ever seen.

"What brings you here?"

"Well, I'm on terminal leave and I thought I'd like to look at some mountains again. I remembered Jimmy liked these."

The old man gestured loosely. "Let's sit on the porch."

Tully stepped aside and the old man slowly came out. He indicated the porch swing, and went on to the worn rocker at the corner of the porch and let himself down slowly. Watching him, Tully felt a wrench of pity. Jimmy had been all the old man had, and for a fleeting moment Tully sensed the ageless tragedy of the childless old. But pity was a luxury Tully wasn't affording at the moment, and he made his expression reserved and pleasant.

"How you feeling, son? I figured from Jimmy's last letter you'd be in the hospital for quite a stretch yet."

"A pair of broken legs isn't much, nowadays."

"They bother you?"

Tully shrugged, faintly embarrassed by the old man's solicitude. "They go numb at unexpected times. Some nerve pinch or something. The doctors couldn't see me flying a plane with them, so I'm out."

The old man nodded. He had never taken his shrewd gaze from Tully's face, and now a kind of unease was in Tully. He had meant to sympathize with the old man, to reminisce about Jimmy, to hear about the military funeral only a month past, to imprint on the old man's mind his affection for Jimmy and his shared sense of loss. But the old man had not even mentioned Jimmy yet.

"How have you been, sir? Jimmy worried about you toward the last." The lie came easily, for it was a lie. Living, Jimmy never thought of his father; dying, he thought of himself.

The old man looked uncomfortable. "I'm all right, Jimmy knew that, and it shouldn't have worried him."

"Need any help?"

The old man looked carefully at him, and his jaw closed firmly. "No sir, and I never have."

Tully felt a faint flush of embarrassment mount to his face, and with it came a sudden caution. *Go easy*, he thought; *get on something safe.* "I suppose it's sort of hard for you to talk about Jimmy, sir, but is there anything you wanted to ask me about him? I was with him from the time we crashed until the end."

The old man asked quietly, "Do you want to talk about it?"

"If you want to hear it."

"That means you don't." He was silent a moment, considering. "Who was the boy who wrote Jimmy's letters for him in the hospital? I'd like to write and thank him."

"I don't know, sir. Jimmy and I were in different wards, although I saw a lot of him. It might have been a nurse." This second lie came even more easily, but as he looked at the old man he thought with a faint stirring of apprehension, *Why does he ask that? Does he know I wrote them?*

"No, it was a man's writing," old Kevin said. "It doesn't matter. I guess I know everything else I need to know."

That'll hold me, Tully thought sardonically. He drew out a pack of cigarettes, offered the pack to Kevin, who declined, and then slowly lighted a smoke. He was wondering why he had ever thought this scheme would work. Not all parents were like the people in stories and books, he was learning again. There were some who accepted the death of their young as stoically as animals, who rejected sympathy, who guarded their feelings with such an iron determination that there was no access to them. Tully had counted on old Kevin's loneliness, his need for sympathy and help, yet the old man needed nothing, and Tully's scheme was no scheme at all.

The old man's voice broke in on his thoughts. "Jimmy wrote you were a mining man, son."

Instantly, Tully's heart began to pound. So the old boy remembered. Here was the chance, the slim chance, and he must handle it with care.

"That's right," he said idly, and he added, "that's about all I know how to do except fly a plane."

"We had quite a camp here once."

Tully nodded. "The Iron Top, and the McClellan. I should say you did, unless all the textbooks lied."

"They didn't lie," old Kevin said softly. "Where've you worked?"

Tully told him he'd been with Anaconda since he left school, that on his last job he'd been loaned out to a subsidiary company doing exploratory work in Aspen, Colorado, on lead-zinc. He'd been there when the Marine Reserve called him up.

"Like these big companies?" old Kevin asked.

Tully shrugged, knowing the old man was feeling him out. "I don't know anything else. Nowadays, you work for them or you mostly don't work."

The old man nodded. "It's a poor profession these days if you're a loner. Going back with them?"

"Yes. After I loaf awhile."

They sat in tranquil silence, and Tully was fairly certain he had passed the first test. It wasn't much, but it was a start. He thought back to the many letters he had written old Kevin pretending they were on behalf of Jimmy, whose arms were rotting with gangrene and whose mind was drugged with pain-killing opiates. Each of those letters always contained news of Lieutenant Gibbs, Jimmy's savior, his friend, his pilot. And each told a little more of Lieutenant Gibbs, how they talked mining, what a swell guy Gibbs was. Tully wondered now if he had overdone it, but he knew he wouldn't know that until later.

Old Kevin stirred then and said, "Well, you picked a good place to loaf. How long you plan to stay?"

"A few days, maybe," Tully said. "I want to do a lot of walking and get my legs back in shape. Then I'd like to look at some of the old mines, too."

"There's a fair-sized one north of town up Liberty Gulch, the Mahaffey. It's a good lead-zinc-silver property."

Tully threw away his cigarette and rose. "I'll see you around, won't I, Mr. Russel?"

"Certainly. I walk to the post office every day and mostly rest in the afternoon. Come over any time you feel like it; in fact, come over lots." He smiled his soft, almost shy smile and rose too. Tully shook his big, flat-palmed callused hand and in parting said, "This is a nice quiet place you have here."

"It suits me."

Back on the road again Tully assessed what he had accomplished. It wasn't much except that he thought the old man liked him on sight. Meanwhile, remembering he mustn't crowd the old boy, he would have to be content with that while he moved as circumspectly as possible.

He had paved the way for this next move by telling old Kevin he wanted to look at the country, which was natural enough for a mining man. Now, cutting back to town across the weed-grown lots, he was ready to go to work.

The town viewed from this distance seemed to shoulder against the very base of the high peaks which ribboned off into numberless gulches whose sides were scarred by the pale wash of old mine dumps. The tallest building in town was the cupolaed brick courthouse, and Tully, picking his way through the back streets, headed for it. Its iron fence guarding the marble monument to the Civil War soldiers and shining in the sunlight was freshly painted. Its lawn was deep emerald green against the faded brick of the courthouse.

Inside, the halls were lofty and dim-lit and smelled of aged wood and well-used cuspidors. The county offices were proclaimed by scroll letters in gold leaf in their solid doors, a mocking memory of the county's wealthier days.

Tully shouldered through the door marked "County Clerk and Recorder," and moved up to the counter that barred his way into the big room. Here was a monumental clutter of papers on old slant-top bookkeepers' desks, but from somewhere in the back of the room came the sound of a typewriter clattering at a terrific pace. Tully looked about him and since the typing continued, he cleared his throat noisily. The typewriter ceased and from around the desk came a girl. It took Tully one careful look to identify her as the girl in the red convertible of last night. It took a longer and an even more careful look for her to identify him as she halted on the far side of the counter.

"Did you get rid of him?" Tully asked.

"At ten minutes to two, no thanks to you," she answered coldly.

Tully shook his head wonderingly. "An old family friend?"

"Not anymore."

Tully said, "What's the matter? Did you forget where you lived? Couldn't you have driven home, thanked him for a nice evening and gone inside?"

"You don't know Ben Hodes," the girl said.

"You tried awfully hard to introduce me," Tully countered dryly. "What was I supposed to do—say hello and kick his head off?"

"If you'd been a gentleman, you wouldn't even have said hello."

Tully felt a thrust of irritation. "If you don't like drunks don't go out with them."

"That's a large order in this town."

"Then you ought to organize a rescue unit and not depend on strangers."

"Especially timid ones."

"Right," Tully said. "Who's in charge here?"

The girl laughed suddenly. "Put down that lorgnette, Duchess. Won't I do?"

"If you're the recorder," Tully said shortly.

"I do his job when he isn't here. What is it you want?"

"I think Kevin and Jimmy Russel have some mining claims in this county. I'd like to know their location."

The girl's slim face altered, a faint suspicion in it now.

"Any special claims, or would just any of the Russel claims do?"

"These are on Officer's Ridge."

The girl's eyebrows raised. "Now how did you know that? It's called Vicksburg Hill now, and only the oldest-timers ever call it Officer's Ridge."

"Why, Jimmy told me."

"Did he tell you to have a look at the claims there?"

Plain annoyance mounted into Tully's face. "He did, but I haven't got an affidavit to prove it."

"Okay, Donald Duck. Sit down and pour yourself a glass of sherry while I hunt up the ledger."

She turned and walked into the big vault in the left wall of the room. Altogether she was a pleasant sight, standing, walking or scolding, Tully thought. He wondered who Ben Hodes was that she and presumably the rest of the town girls were so in awe of him.

Presently she returned with the big ledger, dumped it on the desk and said, "Do you suppose I could ask you a question, a very small one, without having to watch you take your shirt off and fight?"

"Go ahead," Tully said coldly.

"How do you propose to find these claims on Vicksburg?"

"There are corners, aren't there?"

"Have you got a map, a compass, a surveyor and a logging crew in your pocket?"

Tully frowned. "Why, are they hard to find?"

"Unless you know the country, they're impossible. There's no road to them. There are some prospect holes on the claims, but you have to know even your game trails to find them." She added with a faint trace of humor in her tone, "If you're thinking of buying them, I can save you time."

Tully straightened up. "I'm not. Why? Aren't they for sale?"

"There have been offers—none of them accepted."

"Who offered?"

"Ben Hodes for one. He runs the Mahaffey."

Tully said wearily, "There's that man again."

The girl flushed, but said nothing. She started to open the claim ledger when Tully put his hands on the cover. "I guess I don't need that. Can anybody around here take me to the claims?"

The girl thought a moment, then asked, "Do you want to pay for a jeep?" At Tully's nod of assent, she turned and crossed the room to the telephone and dialed a number.

"Alec?" she asked. "This is Sarah Moffit. Are you working today?"

Tully watched her with a close attention as she talked. He had had dealings enough with other county officials to know that they were a mine of miscellaneous information, the importance of which they seldom had an accurate knowledge. He would have liked to ask this Sarah Moffit more about the Vicksburg Claims, but he remembered the caution that mounted into her green eyes when he had first mentioned it.

She turned and asked abruptly, "Can you be ready in half an hour?"

"In ten minutes."

The girl relayed the message and hung up, then crossed back to the counter.

"Your man will pick you up at the hotel in fifteen minutes. His name is Alec Bacchione and he'll bring lunch."

"Sounds like a dude wrangler," Tully observed.

"Not quite," the girl said patiently. "Alec was a combat engineer during the last war, and he's sort of a freelance heavy-equipment operator. For a while he was chainman for the county surveyor, and he's guided hunting parties, too. That's why I picked him, because he knows that country like a book." She added dryly, "You'll be in safe hands. You'd better change out of those dancing pumps, too. You're going to see some country."

Tully looked at her a long moment, then said, "Every time I have an impulse to be polite to you, you change my mind, so I better say thanks before you do it again."

"That's all right. It was only a little trouble." They re-

garded each other with a mild hostility before Tully turned
and went out.

As he changed into rough clothes and engineer boots in
his room, his thoughts kept returning to the girl. She had a
sort of cross-grained, almost malicious way about her that
he did not wholly understand. His rudeness of last night she
had returned to him compounded. Moreover, she met him
with a mingled suspicion and dislike that he was not accus-
tomed to. It was as if without voicing it she suspected his
motives in looking over these claims. *That's small town,* he
thought, *but I've got to be careful. Alec will tell her everything I say.*

A battered army surplus jeep was waiting in front of the
hotel when he stepped out. The man behind the wheel was
dressed in oft-washed coveralls and an ancient ski cap. He
was a short, heavy young man with the dark perceptive eyes
and the almost tender smile of an Italian. He introduced
himself, shook hands with Tully, and gave him a few grudging seconds to throw his packsack on the back seat and
settle himself before he shot the jeep into a U-turn and
headed north out of town and up the valley.

A .22 rifle lay between the separate front seats and Tully,
pulling it away from the gear shifts, asked, "Is a gun stan-
dard equipment in these parts?"

"If you live here," Alec said laconically.

"I don't follow you."

Alec gave him a quick grin. "Ducks and blue grouse."

"Is the season open on them?"

"Only if you live here," Alec said again. Then he glanced
obliquely at Tully and said, "These are our birds and our
game in these mountains, no matter what the state says. We
kill them whenever we want but never for fun. That's more
than these jokers from Kansas or Nebraska with their hunting licenses can say, isn't it?"

Tully grinned too. "Right you are," and thought sourly, *A
character.*

Only a few minutes from town the main traveled road
turned left up a gulch. A sign at the forks pointing left said

"Mahaffey Mines, Inc." Alec's way was straight ahead and the road, an abandoned mine road, was already scarcely more than a track. It climbed into black spruce and twisted through alders fringing the creek which they were to ford twenty more times in the next two hours.

Against the grinding of the gears and the noisy jolting of the jeep, conversation was impossible. Tully knew that Alec was wondering at the reasons for this trip and sooner or later he would have to be satisfied, but at the moment his silence was welcome and Tully reviewed the little he knew of the Russel Claims.

Most of it had been gleaned in the long days and nights Jimmy and he had lain side by side on the schoolhouse floor. They'd been brought there after the crash of their Tigercat F7F on the rocky beach to the east.

To dull their pain they talked, forgetting their dislike of each other. The one thing they had in common, an interest in mining, had never been a bond between them; Jimmy's contempt for a "schoolbook miner" had seen to that. But during those interminable and miserable days Jimmy swallowed his prejudice, and he talked about little else but the Officer's Ridge or Vicksburg Claims, ten in number, that were so rich in lead, zinc and silver. Every man had a dream in his heart, and these claims were Jimmy's dream. Neither Jimmy nor his father could raise the money to develop them, Jimmy had told him. The R.F.C. Mining Loan Department had rejected their application for a government loan on the grounds that federal money was intended to enlarge going properties and not to develop prospects.

As for raising outside money, it was the old story that Tully knew so well. There is nothing quite so articulate and hopelessly optimistic as a miner trying to share his deep conviction that there is great mineral wealth on claims he owns. The rest of the story was classic in its outline. Other mining interests knew the worth of the claims, but they also knew old Kevin's inability to develop them. Insulting offers had been insultingly rejected.

The substitute for a road which they had been traveling

now hauled up abruptly at a caved-in cabin among the spruce. A tunnel mouth opened jaggedly into the slope behind the shack and Alec put the jeep across the rusting tram rails toward the other side of the clearing saying, "From here on we bushwhack."

The jeep climbed more steeply now and under Alec's guiding hand it seemed to be almost sentient, picking its way around windfalls and choosing passages through the thinning timber that were just wide enough to accommodate it. A startled buck off to Tully's right watched them in still amazement for long seconds, and then went vaulting off down the hill.

They were presently in a thicket of young aspens and Alec hesitated just long enough to put the jeep into low low. Then he butted through the thicket, bending down the trees ahead of him, and soon they broke out onto a high grassy bench interspersed with heavy thickets of black spruce which they traveled for another hour.

Looking ahead, Tully had guessed that this bench would take them by gradual ascent to a higher craggy ridge looming directly ahead of them and nestled below the high peaks, but this was not to be. Only minutes later Alec swung the jeep in a half circle, cut the motor and said, "End of the line. It drops straight off past the edge of the timber."

They shrugged into their packsacks and Tully surprised Alec covertly watching him as he adjusted his straps.

"There's ten claims strung out in a line on top of that ridge," Alec said, pointing. "Where do you want to head for?"

"Claims three and four."

"Sarah tell you what's on them?"

Tully shook his head. "Jimmy did. That's where the fault lies closest to the surface, isn't it?"

Alec nodded slowly. "So I heard, but I never heard *him* say it."

Something in his voice held Tully's attention and they regarded each other almost with hostility.

"He didn't talk much about them?"

"Not to me."

"You weren't a POW with him," Tully said quietly. "You talk about a lot of funny things when there's not much else to talk about."

Alec said matter-of-factly, "Yes, I heard Jimmy's pilot was in town. You going to mine this?"

He heard it from the cook, of course, Tully thought with a feeling of self-derision. How could you keep any secret in a town the size of Azurite? Here was his chance to spike all the rumors for once and all. He laughed shortly, without humor. "Do I look like Daddy Warbucks? No, I'm a miner by trade. I've been in a hospital seventeen weeks. I came to see old Kevin and I thought I'd take a look at these claims Jimmy told me about. Just call it a day in the country if it'll make you feel any better."

Alec blushed slightly and shrugged. "It's okay by me. Why shouldn't it be?" He hunched his packsack higher on his shoulders and set off toward the timber. Tully followed him down a steep game trail into a valley that seemed as deep as the Grand Canyon. They crossed a willow slough which left their legs covered with stinking mud up to the knees and then began their assault on Vicksburg Hill.

It was a grueling climb that was a cross between straight mountain-climbing and a logging operation. Tully had never seen small timber so thick nor cliffs of rotten rocks so precipitous. Alec with his small hand axe hacked and chopped his way through the tangle. He held a pace that left Tully's legs rubbery and his chest heaving for wind.

Once atop the ridge, Tully threw himself on the ground utterly beat while Alec rolled a smoke and patiently regarded the country and, alternately, his companion. When Tully had recovered enough to sit up, he began to note the geology of the ridge. It was made up of decomposed granite and porphyry with occasional outcroppings of rotten quartz. When Alec saw him stirring again, he rose and wordlessly set off on a course due west through sparse, wind-twisted spruce. A five minutes' walk along the far side of the ridge brought them to the Russel workings, and here Alec halted and said, "Here's one. There's another a half mile further on."

A discovery shaft, a tripod of timbers for a hoist above it, had been sunk into the rotten rock. But before descending, Tully first scouted the area and picked up signs of the fissure vein. Then halting, he shrugged off his packsack, opened it and brought out a prospector's pick and miner's lamp and then moved toward the shaft. A small dump of country rock, the useless non-ore-bearing rock, lay beyond it, separated from a dump of the true ore-bearing rock.

"Want to go along?"

Alec shook his head in negation. "My old man spent his life in one of them. I'm never going to spend an hour in one."

There was a persistent breeze from the west at this altitude that chilled Tully and made the shelter of the shaft welcome. The ladder was in good condition but he descended carefully, turning his lamp on the walls of the shaft. Three quarters of the way down, at fifteen feet, he picked up the first traces of the zinc and lead outcrop. Where the drill holes had scarred the rock surface, he saw the shiny jet crystals of galena-lead. As he descended, he saw the vein widening until, standing in the foot of icy water at the bottom of the shaft, the whole structure of the vein lay before him. Sulphides of silver and zinc in addition to the galena mottled the walls which were slate gray and appeared to be almost solid ore-bearing rock. Slow excitement welled up within him as he shone his lamp on walls and ceiling. Jimmy Russel, even in delirium, had not exaggerated the quantity exposed.

Presently, he sloshed back ten feet into the tunnel. The tunnel ran for only a few feet before it ended. The showings all along the way were uniform and when he halted at the face of the drift which did not even expose the whole vein, it came to him with a stunning force that if Jimmy's smelter report figures were right, old man Russel had a fortune in his hands—a fortune he was powerless to touch.

The cold water had numbed his feet through his boots,

but still Tully did not move. He was calculating the labor it had cost for the imperfect exploratory work Jimmy had accomplished. All the ore, after being blasted and hoisted out, had probably been sacked and packed by mule down to a shipping point for milling and smelting, a monumental task. Jimmy's only reward had been a set of figures on a smelter report, but that had been reward enough, Tully knew. He turned now and retraced his steps, climbing the shaft ladder into the pushing wind of the sunny afternoon. He hoped, as he walked toward Alec, that the lingering excitement he still felt did not show in his face.

Alec had chosen a seat behind a rock out of the wind and Tully slacked down behind him and they ate their lunch. Presently, Alec regarded his soggy boots and said, "At least you got the mud washed off. What was it like?"

"It's there. What it'll run, I don't know," Tully said matter-of-factly. "What did old Kevin and Jimmy ever do with it?"

"Just what you see. They packed samples down from here and from the other discovery shaft and that's about all."

"Is it good enough to mine on this market?" Tully said.

"The way I get it, to make a mine pay you've got to haul out ore; to haul out ore you got to have a road." He glanced at Tully and said dryly, "I understand roads don't come cheap in this stuff."

Tully nodded. "A big outfit could swing it though."

"Old Kevin isn't big. And again, the way I get it, the big outfits want all of it if they put in the road."

Tully scowled, "What about the county?"

"What about it?"

"I mean if the county takes a look at what Kevin's got, they should build a road so he can open up his mine. The taxes they'd get from his operations would easily pay for the road."

"Ha!" Alec said bitterly. "Maybe some other county but not this one."

Tully looked at him inquiringly. Alec's expression, now

taciturn, seemed to indicate that he thought he had talked too much.

But Tully persisted. "What's the matter with this county? A friend of yours works for it."

Alec glanced quickly at him. "Sarah Moffit? Sure, she's got to live, just like the rest of us."

"You mean if there were any other way to live she wouldn't work for the county?"

"Check."

"I get the feeling behind what you're saying, but I don't understand it," Tully said. "The county won't build Kevin a road. Right?"

Alec nodded.

"Why not?"

"Well, who okays the roads? The commissioners, don't they? You don't have to go any further."

"What have the commissioners got against Kevin?"

Alec smiled almost secretly. "He's a miner and that's enough."

Tully scowled. "Make it plainer."

"Well, during the Depression this town practically folded up. It was the ranchers down the valley who paid all the taxes and who elected the county officials. The three commissioners are ranchers. If there is any dough for roads, they're ranch roads, not mine roads."

Tully shook his head slowly. "That's kind of tough on Kevin."

Alec shrugged. "They tell me that's what the Germans found out under Hitler."

Tully was silent a long moment considering this information. It seemed unreasonable that three county commissioners would vote against something that would add enormously to the tax rolls, but there the facts were.

Alec waited until Tully was finished with his smoke and then said, "Want to look at the other hole?"

For answer Tully rose and Alec took off along the ridge. A quarter of a mile west they came to the second Russel workings. These were not as extensive but showed ore just as rich. It was a reasonable assumption that all along the fissure between the two workings, and no one knew how far west of the second, about the same quantity and grade of ore could exist.

When Tully was through with his look, he joined Alec again, but this time he did not sit down. Standing before Alec, he asked, "Is the timber on that slope we came up as thick everywhere as it was at that spot?"

"Not everywhere. Why?"

Tully said, "I'm just curious. Let me go ahead going back. I'm going to try and hold a twelve percent grade on the way down."

Alec caught it immediately and grinned. "You building the road already?"

Tully shrugged. "It wouldn't be the first one I've built. I'm just curious, is all."

Alec passed the hand axe over to him and rose, and Tully set out in the lead.

Because of the grade Tully held to, the descent was not difficult. As he moved down, he mentally noted the places that would need powder work, but for the most part he observed the road could be built with a bulldozer and a minimum of shoring with timber at hand. When they reached the bottom of the gully a mile below the point at which the jeep was parked, Tully hauled up and said, "Now you find the jeep."

Alec regarded him inquiringly. "How did it look?"

"Well, it'd take money, all right—money nobody's got, I guess."

Darkness overtook them when they were just short of the caved-in shack and the remainder of the ride back to town chilled them both. As they pulled up in front of the hotel, Tully said, "Got time for a drink? Maybe two?"

"Always," Alec said.

"Lead the way."

Alec swung his leg over the side of the jeep and Tully climbed out. He could feel the telltale signs in his tired legs and he prayed silently, *Please, not now.* The bar was next to the hotel entrance and part of the hotel. It was an old-fashioned saloon with tile floor and light maple-wood back bar. Booths were a modern addition and Tully, with kind of panicky haste, headed straight for the closest one. Alec, cutting for the bar, observed Tully's course and changed his own.

Tully sank onto the seat and said, "That was quite a walk for a city boy. I've got to sit down." He could feel the numbness creeping down his legs and a small triumph was in him. He had made it and nobody noticed it.

Alec slid into the seat opposite him. "That was a long walk even for a country boy."

The bartender took their orders and afterwards Tully looked about the room. A scattering of men stood at the bar and at the far end facing the door, arm on the bar top, was the man Tully had seen with Sarah Moffit last night—Ben Hodes.

They looked at each other briefly and then Tully's attention was diverted by Alec's talking to him.

"It looks like some of the boys are getting an early start."

"For what?" Tully asked.

"The dance tonight at the Elks." Then he grinned at Tully. "Want to come?"

"I'm not an Elk."

"I am, and you'll be my guest."

"Sounds good," Tully said.

At that moment the waiter approached with the drinks. Tully ordered another round of the same, and when the waiter was gone he and Alec hoisted their glasses.

"Here's to crime," Tully said.

"By the county commissioners," Alec said. And they drank.

All feeling in Tully's legs was gone by now, and oddly it was a pleasant sensation. In a few minutes, according to past performance, they would be all right again, with nobody the wiser. He was slapping his pockets for a pack of cigarettes when he saw Alec glance up and at the same moment he heard sharp footsteps on the tile floor advancing. Looking

up he saw the towering figure of Ben Hodes halted beside
the booth.

"Hello, Ben," Alec said not very enthusiastically.

Hodes didn't bother to answer; he was looking at Tully
and his heavy, handsome face was scowling. He wore the
stained leather jacket and muddy boots of a working miner,
but Tully noticed that his big hands were clean and uncal-
lused and he thought, *Who's he kidding?*

"Aren't you the joker I talked to last night?" Hodes demanded.

Alec cut in swiftly, "Lay off, Ben. You never saw him in
your life before."

"Ask him."

"Has he?" Alec asked Tully.

"If he could see last night, he did," Tully said. He wondered what was coming.

"Look," Hodes said heavily, "Sarah is no pickup. Get
that through your head right now."

"I never thought she was."

"Then what the hell were you doing annoying her at the
courthouse this morning?"

Faint anger touched Tully. "Who said I was?"

"Never mind, you were seen at her office."

"Annoying her?"

"Don't get salty, friend," Hodes said levelly. "I'm Mr.
Trouble himself if you're looking for him."

A wild anger rose in Tully then and, unthinkingly, he put
both hands on the edge of the table to lunge erect, but he
had forgotten his legs wouldn't respond. He settled back
into his seat, his lips white with anger, and he was aware
suddenly of both Hodes and Alec watching him.

Hodes laughed softly. "What's the matter? Did you take a
second look and change your mind?"

Hodes's jibe combined with the embarrassed look in
Alec's dark eyes brought a blush to Tully's face.

"No, I didn't change my mind. I picked up a pair of
broken legs a while back. When I'm tired they cave in on
me. They've caved right now. I can't stand."

"Nice timing," Hodes observed.

The approach of the waiter with the second round of drinks eased the tension. The waiter said, "You've got a highball cooling down there, Ben. Want me to bring it up here?"

Hodes grunted. "I like it better where I was."

He turned and tramped back down the tile floor to his place at the end of the bar.

Tully paid for the drinks and only then looked at Alec. Alec wouldn't look at him. Tully knew then that Alec didn't believe him, that Alec believed he'd ducked the fight.

2

After a lonely supper at the same restaurant in which he had eaten last night, Tully moved out into the street. Alec had said he would pick him up at nine o'clock and there was time to spare. He stepped out into the town's quiet Saturday night and walked slowly down the cracked sidewalks, his course aimless and time-killing. An occasional car hurried past and couples, arm in arm, called to each other across the street on their way to the party.

Tully's mood was foul. Try as he might he could not shake the memory of the scene in the barroom, and of Alec's shame-filled eyes. Each time he remembered it, he silently cursed his injury. The sudden pleasant friendship with Alec was ended now. He knew this was an unintelligent, uncivilized and adolescent conclusion, but that was the way the world was. He would have to accept it. Put in different words, he supposed that it was every man's duty to fight a bully even if he had to take a beating. He thought this and he knew Alec thought this—and he also knew Hodes thought this, which was what galled him most.

He tried to put his unpleasantness from his mind and think of what he had accomplished today. At the moment it seemed little enough and only added to his depression. Kevin had a prospect, all right, but Tully Gibbs didn't have any part of it and he wouldn't have.

His circle around the block brought him to the hotel door. Looking through the glass, he saw Alec seated in one of the wide lounge chairs. Alec saw him, rose and came out. Sight of him gave Tully a sudden lift of spirits, for Alec was transformed. His sports jacket was a shouting green of four-inch herringbone; paler green slacks were matched by a wallpaper tie of the same tint and Tully knew Alec's clothes were a pretty fair estimate of himself. His own outfit of dark slacks and blue flannel jacket seemed sedate and colorless beside that of his smaller friend.

"What, no girl?" Tully asked.

Alec made an engaging grimace and said, "Too early to pick yet. When I look them over, I'll have one."

They headed upstreet and Alec was full of talk about the dance, the orchestra, the club rooms, the weather, the night —in fact he talked of everything except the day together and the incident with Hodes. *He'll never mention it,* Tully thought grimly.

The Elks club rooms were on the first floor of the big brick building in the center of the next block upstreet. The ballroom—the converted lodge meeting room—was to the left of the entrance, but Alec passed it with barely a glance and led Tully down the corridor to the small bar at the rear. The barroom was jammed with couples and Tully was introduced to a dozen of them before they reached the bar.

His highball was half finished when the orchestra started playing. The barroom emptied except for a few stags, and presently Alec said, "Want to go in?" They went back to the ballroom which was decorated in a harvest motif. Here Tully joined the stag line and had his look at the girls. He cut in on one of the married ones he had met in the barroom, had a sedate turn around the room before he was cut in on, and fell back in the line beside Alec.

Suddenly he caught sight of Sarah Moffit. She was dancing with Ben Hodes, but it took Tully several seconds to realize it, since he looked only at her. Her gown was black and clung in the right places and she had done something to her hair which Tully couldn't immediately identify. He never did; he just liked her figure, which he would have described to someone else as slim, long-legged, just top-heavy enough, and with a beautiful face.

Hodes's presence didn't register immediately. When it did, Tully dismissed it and headed across the floor. He touched Hodes's elbow and said the required words, looking meanwhile at Sarah.

Her smile at sight of him was a forgiving one. He saw Hodes's arm tighten about her as he half turned away, as if refusing to give her up. Sarah, however, moved determinedly out of Hodes's arms and into Tully's and they danced away, leaving Hodes standing sullenly for a long moment in the middle of the floor before he sought the door.

Tully said, "What have you done to your hair?"

Sarah looked up at him, almost startled. "Do you like it?"

"Sure. What am I saying? I liked it before."

"You're much more pleasant than you were this morning," Sarah said.

"That was my business scowl."

"Business?"

She had picked up the word instantly and Tully inwardly cursed his slip of the tongue. "Maybe you don't call a fifteen-mile hike straight up in the air business, but I do. You know—business, like gangsters, meaning let's give the guy the 'business.' "

Sarah smiled. "Did you look at the claims?"

Tully nodded. "Yes, I guess they're all Jimmy thought they were."

"You talk as if you knew."

"I'm a miner by trade."

Sarah was quiet a moment. Tully was beginning to appreciate what an expert dancer she was when she said, "Do you mind if I ask an impertinent question?"

Tully said he didn't.

"Are you going to help Kevin?"

Go easy, Tully thought. *Remember she's Hodes's girl.* "Does he need help? He looks like a pretty rugged character to me."

"Oh, I don't mean that, I mean are you going to help him mine it?"

Tully held her away from him for a free second so that she could see the mock surprise in his eyes. "What gave you that idea?"

"Jimmy's letters to Kevin, for one thing. More than once he wrote that he was going to bring you home with him when he got well." She smiled faintly. "I've read them, so I know."

Tully felt a creeping shame within him, and he thought *More than once I wrote, you mean.* "That's news to me," he said uncomfortably, aware that she was still watching him. He drew her to him, so that she could not see his face, and went on. "No, I came to see old Kevin because Jimmy asked me to. It's kind of a holiday, too. Jimmy had told me about the claims, and being a miner, I wanted a look."

There was a kind of relief in Sarah's voice as she said, "I suppose that's reasonable."

Tully had control of himself now. "Why, are you a friend of old Mr. Russel's?"

"The best."

"And you want to protect him from me?"

The music stopped and Sarah stood before him, a slight frown on her face. "Maybe. I—I just don't know what you want, is all."

Tully grinned swiftly. "Another dance from you later."

The crowd moved off the floor, Tully and Sarah with them. Sarah halted by the door and spoke to a passing couple. Tully waited until they were out of earshot and then said, "I'm trying to add up a few things, but I can't seem to get the right answer."

Sarah looked at him inquiringly and Tully went on, "Remember last night when you wanted to get away from that big, bad man?"

Sarah nodded.

"Remember this morning when he was mentioned again?"

Sarah was watching him and did not answer.

"They both add up to a date with him tonight. That's what I'm trying to figure out."

Sarah said, "Have you looked at the men here?"

"Sure. What's the matter with them?" he asked, and began shaking his head.

"Why are you doing that?"

"You're going to say something I'll hate you for, but go ahead."

"Well, isn't he more attractive than any of them?"

Tully snorted, "If I were a buffalo hunter, I might think so."

Sarah laughed, but Tully regarded her soberly and said, "That's no answer."

"Well, I can handle him, where other girls can't," Sarah said with a kind of mockery in her voice. "He's a change from dusty ledgers. He's exciting, too. Have you ever thought what fun it might be to go everywhere with a not very tame gorilla? It's wrong, but it's fun to watch him scare people; it's exciting to watch him break things; it's fun to watch him get exactly what he wants in the most direct way. If he ever had a thought, it would injure his brain. Every time I go out with him, I manage to forget that 1910 typewriter waiting for me in the office."

"That's still no answer."

"All right, he likes me. He's not bad looking, he dresses well, he's almost civilized and he's got a standing in the community, like it or not. Besides that, we grew up together and I understand him. If you could find twenty other men in town you could say the same things about, I'd go out with them."

"I wish you would."

Sarah only laughed. "Don't take him so seriously. I don't."

Tully sighed. "Well, the Chinese have opium and you have him."

The music started again just as Sarah laughed. Tully put a hand on her elbow and steered her toward the floor, a kind of bafflement on his face. She'd been frank. He had halted and Sarah was coming into his arms when he felt a rough hand on his elbow. He was half spun around by the force of it and was brought up facing Hodes. Ben had his other hand on Sarah's elbow and now he said, "I want to buy you two kids a drink. Come on."

Tully removed Hodes's hand from his arm gently but firmly, and Hodes seemed willing enough to let go of him. Tully glanced at Sarah, who said, "Oh Lord, that will make seven Cokes since we got here."

Hodes looked almost genially at Tully. "Come along."

Hodes and Sarah moved down the corridor ahead of Tully, and he wondered what was coming. There was a kind of animal jauntiness in Hodes's gait and in his broad shoulders.

The bar held only a few couples, and Hodes gently propelled Sarah to one of the leather-covered seats. Tully sat on one side of her and faced Hodes, who sat on the other side across the table.

Hodes said presently, "I don't want a drink and neither does Junior here, Sarah. I just want to talk." Elbow on the table, he raised a big fist, extended a thick finger and pointed it at Tully. "Break out your hearing aid, Junior, I'm going to say it all over again."

"Say what all over again?" Sarah asked.

"I told this character this afternoon you were no pickup. Now he's trying it again."

Sarah looked at Tully, who was watching Hodes with a still attentiveness. Tully did not look at her. He leaned both elbows on the table and said, "Has anyone ever called you a slob? Because if they haven't, I am now."

A kind of delight welled up in Hodes's dark eyes. "Lots of people, Junior, but only once."

"You're a slob. That's twice for me."

Sarah said softly, "Oh, Lord."

Hodes leaned back in his chair and glanced amusedly at Sarah, but he spoke to Tully. "Every time I wreck a place she won't give me a date for ten days. Have you any objection to the night air?"

Tully stood up. "Not at all. May I have this dance, Mr. Hodes?"

Ben laughed and stood up, too, a look of animal pleasure in his eyes.

Sarah said imploringly to both of them, "I wish you wouldn't. Please, please, don't!" She looked now at Ben. "Beth is right there at the bar, Ben. Don't do it."

Tully glanced over his shoulder and saw a slight, dark-skinned girl wearing a pale blue dress in conversation with a bespectacled, balding man. They were at the far end of the bar, but even at this distance Tully could see that Beth must be Hodes's sister. He felt Sarah's hand on his arm and looked back at her.

"Please don't," she begged.

Tully said, "Remember? It's fun to watch him scare people." He waited until he saw the deep flush rise into her face and then he turned and followed Hodes into the corridor.

There was a door at the back of the hallway that led out into a cinder-strewn alley. The light above the door cast a bright and wide circle of light. Hodes halted in the alley and looked at Tully. "How's this? These cinders will probably dirty your shirt, but so would a barroom floor." He was methodically shucking out of his expensive sports coat which he tossed on a trash crate beside the door.

Tully stripped out of his coat and said, "Why don't we make this for something besides fun?"

"You sound like a money fighter, Junior," Hodes said affably. "Sure. What'll it be?"

"Got any money in your bank here?" Tully asked.

"I'm the majority stockholder."

"Okay," Tully said. "You lose and you go on my note for a ten-thousand, one-hundred-and-twenty-day loan."

Hodes said swiftly, "That's a deal—half of it anyway. What are you putting up?"

"Why naturally—the thing you seem to want—I won't see Sarah again."

Hodes snorted angrily. "That's a hell of a bet."

"That's what we're fighting over, isn't it?"

Hodes scowled, trying to pin down Tully's glibness. Tully was remembering Sarah's words, *If he ever had a thought, it would injure his brain.* Liquor, excitement and his naturally slow process of thought had Hodes confused for a moment and now Tully taunted him, "Make up your mind, I'm getting cold. Besides, you'd probably welsh on the bet."

Hodes lowered his head. "Junior, we're talking too much. Let's make it that bet and get to work."

"What are we waiting for?" He stepped out toward Hodes, and with a delighted shout Hodes rushed in.

Tully crouched and in a driving block took Ben just above the knees, raising his back as he felt contact. Hodes's feet, with no grip on the cinders and propelled by Tully's weight, rose higher than his head as he sailed over Tully's back. He tried to break his fall, failed and landed heavily on his shoulder and face in the cinders. A great grunt escaped him.

Tully was standing, hands at his side when Hodes came to his feet. Hodes lifted his shoulder and ducked his head to wipe the cinders from his cheek and then, almost as an afterthought, he looked at the shoulder of his white shirt. There was blood on it. Slowly he swiveled his glance to Tully, who said mockingly, "You're clumsy, chum. No cigar for that try."

A low animal sound of anger rose in Hodes's throat and he came in, this time cautiously for the first few steps and then recklessly. Tully landed a blow in his face, rode with it inside his guard and gave him a shoulder in the chest before he stepped nimbly aside and clouted Hodes on his ear with the flat of his palm as Hodes lunged past.

Hodes wheeled and again charged, arms windmilling, his breath coming in labored sighs.

Tully knew that he was outweighed a good thirty pounds and that Hodes had a reach of many inches on him. He knew, too, that if he cut up Hodes's face, the man's vanity would push him to murder sooner or later. It was his broad unprotected belly that Tully aimed for then; his left hand was in the crook of Hodes's elbow, and it checked the swing long enough for him to pivot inside against the bigger man's body. He lifted a driving right into the middle of Hodes's white shirt front and at the same time, he felt the jarring impact of Hodes's face on the point of his shoulder.

He broke away swiftly, ducking Hodes's reaching bear hug, and Hodes, thinking his man was evading him again, charged stubbornly.

Tully's halt was too quick for him; Hodes walked face first into Tully's locked and straightened left arm and it halted him with an abruptness that straightened out his knees. Tully saw his opening again and drove a wild, chancy right with all his might and anger behind it into Hodes's belly. At the moment of impact, he caught Hodes's round-house swing on his head. It knocked him flat and with head ringing, he rolled over on the cinders and was immediately on his feet.

But Hodes was down flat on his back, arms wrapped around his belly, knees almost touching his chin. He was gagging for air with an ugly sobbing noise. Tully walked over to him and was only then aware of Sarah Moffit standing against the closed corridor door. Tully said harshly, "Get back in there, you fool!"

A startled look came into Sarah's eyes and she obeyed swiftly, and now Tully put his attention to Hodes. The big man rolled over on his knees and retched and presently came unsteadily to his feet, his back to Tully.

"Turn around, chum!" Tully said sharply.

Hodes wheeled heavily, his feet outspread to brace himself. His cut lip and myriad scratches on his face were bleeding, and now he wiped his cheek on his shirt with that same gesture of raising his shoulder. At sight of Tully standing relaxed and unmarked save for a smear of dirt across the right sleeve and front of his shirt, a sick discouragement was in Hodes's eyes. His chest was heaving with his continuous effort to breathe.

He and Tully watched each other for still seconds and then Tully said, "You can always walk away from it, you know."

Hodes felt a trickle of blood on his chin and he scraped it

off with a slow angry gesture of his palm, but he made no move toward Tully. For ten long seconds Hodes regarded him, a baffled hatred in his eyes. Then, wordlessly he walked over to his coat, lifted it on his arm and walked out of the circle of lamp light into the darkness of the alley.

Wearily Tully tramped over and picked up his own coat and shrugged into it. He heard the corridor door open and Beth Hodes stepped out. She closed the door behind her and looked up and down the alley and finally at Tully. "Where is he?" she asked softly.

Tully inclined his head in the direction Hodes had taken and said nothing.

"Are you hurt?" Beth asked.

Tully said curtly, "Ask him," wheeled and walked down the alley toward the hotel.

Sarah watched her Sunday School class scatter with subdued whoops down the musty basement corridor of the church, and then she glanced up through the unwashed window at the drizzle of rain outside. She suddenly made up her mind that there would be no sermon for her today. The church would be cold, smelling of wet wool and shoe polish, and she lacked the tranquillity of spirit needed for the next hour.

On the church steps she raised her gay umbrella and resignedly breasted the tide of incoming churchgoers who greeted her with mild disapproval in their glances. Turning toward the business district and her apartment, she felt her spirits lift. Black Mountain ahead of her was shrouded in leaden clouds, and great mares' tails of rain drifted down New York Gulch, but she had escaped the confining hour. Underfoot, the sidewalk was washed clean and the air was heavy with the smell of earth and wet leaves.

A half block ahead of her, Sarah saw her mother approaching. She was erect and in a hurry, lest she be late for the service, but in her haste she had not forgotten that she was wearing her best hat, Sarah noticed, and her umbrella was low.

She seemed a little surprised to see Sarah, and halted.

"I'm a renegade this morning, Ma," Sarah announced.

"Well, I put the roast in at quarter to eleven. You can fix the potatoes if you want."

"How big's the roast?"

Mrs. Moffit looked at her daughter carefully. Sarah knew her mother had been a beautiful girl once, and some of what made up that beauty—friendliness and understanding—was in her expression now. "Tremendous," she announced. "Who's it to be besides Kevin?"

"Sam, maybe, and maybe someone else, not Ben."

"Well, that's a comfort," Mrs. Moffit said, and then added hastily, "Without his appetite, we're sure to have enough."

Her mother's near slip brought a smile to Sarah's face. She said, "You better hurry, Ma," and they parted. Mrs. Moffit did not like Ben Hodes; she hadn't liked him since he was a boy, although wild horses couldn't have dragged this admission from her, Sarah knew. She also knew that her mother, in spite of all reassurances to the contrary from Sarah, was afraid that Sarah was serious about Ben.

The Moffit apartment was in the heart of the business district over Benbow's furniture store. Five years ago, a year after her father's death, Sarah and her mother had decided that the old Hawley house, a relic of the boom days inherited by Mrs. Moffit from her father, was no place for two women. They had exchanged its cavernous rooms, its heavy furniture, its wide lawn—none of which they could afford to keep up—for this spacious apartment. Between Sarah's courthouse job and Mrs. Moffit's library job, they lived comfortably.

Sarah climbed the stairs swiftly and let herself in, then halted abruptly inside the door. *What's my hurry?* she wondered, as she strolled across the living room, slowly drawing off her gloves. Suddenly, she realized she was walking straight toward the phone stand. She sat on its chair, looking at the room. The furniture was new, modern but not daffy, and as bright as the day outside was dark, and suddenly she felt good and assured.

She made three phone calls then, one to Alec Bacchione asking him to pick up Kevin and deliver him here at one. The second call was to Sam Horne, editor and owner of the weekly *Azurite Nugget*. Before she made the third call, she lit a cigarette and stared thoughtfully across the room at the Picabia print on the far wall, aware suddenly that she might be heading straight for trouble.

Then she called the hotel and asked for Mr. Gibbs.

She had a moment's wait while the clerk mounted to the second floor, and during that moment she almost hung up. This was foolish and pushing, she thought, and then she thought sternly, *No it isn't, it's a peace offering.*

"Hello." Tully's voice held reserve, almost suspicion.

"This is that damned fool you wouldn't let into the alley last night," Sarah said.

"Oh. How are you?" Still reserved.

"You took the very words out of my mouth."

"Are you checking for your friend? If you are, tell him I had a good night's sleep and I'm in the pink."

"He can't wait to hear," Sarah said sweetly. She paused. "Are we through being nasty to each other? Because if we are, how would you like to have Sunday dinner with us?"

"Us?"

"Not Ben and me. Mother and Kevin and Sam Horne and me. Can't you smell the roast?"

"Wonderful," Tully said. "Thank you very much."

"Come early—in about half an hour. I've got a couple of recipes I want to swap with you."

She hung up, wondering what had prompted her to ask him to come early. She thought she knew. She wanted to ask him questions that he could not answer in front of the others.

She was busy in the kitchen preparing the potatoes when she heard the doorbell. She wiped her dripping hands on her apron, took a look at the unfinished work, and then knew she couldn't pretend to be the leisurely hostess.

She did not remove her apron before she opened the door and stepped aside, holding out her hand. "Hi, Tully. Come in." As he shook hands, she said, "Oh, heavens. How did you find us? I forgot to give you directions."

Tully grinned faintly and shrugged out of his dripping topcoat. "The town's not that big, is it?" he observed.

Sarah took his coat and hung it in the closet, and Tully looked around the gay room. "Who'd have thought it?" he murmured. "This is nice." Then they both looked at each other, and Sarah saw the carefully concealed wariness in his pale eyes. But she liked his face. A little too thin, maybe, and his nose looked as though it might have been broken long ago. Somehow, it communicated a wonderful self-reliance without showing any cockiness or arrogance.

"Still mad?" she asked.

"I never was—at you."

"Good. Come along and help. Ma's at church and I'm cook."

She led him down the corridor between the two bedrooms and out into the kitchen where she pointed to a stool in the corner. "Take the easy chair. Do you like martinis?"

Tully was slow in answering, and she turned to surprise a look of puzzlement on his face. "Sure."

"Want to make some?"

"I thought you drank Cokes—seven, to be exact, last night."

"That's just on Saturday night. Everybody drinks on Saturday night by appointment, as if it were a ritual. I just don't like to be told when I want a drink, when maybe I don't want it. That's not the idea of alcohol, is it?"

"I guess not," Tully said, and he grinned in agreement.

Sarah pointed to the liquor cabinet and Tully busied himself making a shaker of martinis. Sarah was aware that he was watching her as she worked, as if he were a little uncertain about her and this invitation, too. Once she had everything under control, she turned to him and said, "Want to go in the living room?"

"I like it here," Tully said. They sat down in the spacious dining alcove and Tully poured their drinks.

Sarah raised her glass. "Here's to crime."

They both drank to that, and then Tully asked idly, "Have fun last night?"

"As a matter of fact I did. Once Ben went home, I got awfully popular." She laughed shortly. "Maybe the boys ought to retain you for the Elks dances."

Tully reached in the breast pocket of his sports jacket and pulled out a big cigar. A red ribbon was tied around it. "I found that in my box this morning. The clerk said Alec Bacchione left it."

They both laughed at that. Sarah sipped her drink, wondering how to bring the conversation around to where she wanted it, when Tully did it for her.

"Did I hear you say old Kevin was coming for dinner?" At her nod, he asked, "Is that on my account?"

"Partly—except that he comes almost every Sunday. That way, we can be sure he has at least one decent meal a week."

"But why partly on my account?"

"Well, you came here to see him, didn't you?"

Tully nodded.

"Then, too," Sarah went on, "I want to be around when you talk mining to him."

Tully scowled. "Last night, you didn't want me to."

"I still don't—but I know you will."

Tully slowly turned the martini glass on the table top, and he regarded her with quiet belligerence. "Look here. What's the matter with me? What have I done wrong?"

"Nothing. Only you don't add up," Sarah said quietly. "For instance, how well did you know Jimmy Russel?"

"As well as a pilot knows his radarman. As well as you'd know anyone you were in trouble with."

"Did you like him?"

She saw a swift calculation rise in Tully's pale eyes. "No," he said.

"Yet you got a Silver Star for pulling him out of a flaming plane when both your legs were broken."

Tully scowled. "Who told you that?"

"The honor guard at Jimmy's funeral."

Tully shrugged, and Sarah watched him begin to light a

cigarette with care, then remembered her and offered her one. She took one, and he lighted both his and hers, then leaned back against the wall.

"Whether I liked him had nothing to do with that. You'd pull a mad dog out of a burning plane before you'd let that happen to him."

"I can see that," Sarah agreed. "Still, I can't see you coming to this remote spot and looking up Jimmy's father. You'd do it for a friend, but would you do it for someone you didn't like?"

"I have," Tully said shortly.

"That's what I mean. Why?"

Tully shrugged, and glanced thoughtfully out the window at the slow drizzle. When his glance returned to hers, Sarah saw an added sharpness to it.

"How well did *you* know Jimmy?" he asked.

"Very well. He was the most detestable brat, the worst son and most contemptible creature I've ever known. His mother died when he was born. Kevin had to work and still try and raise him. The neighbors took turns, and one by one they gave up. He stole, he lied, and he bullied. By the time he was fourteen Kevin couldn't lick him anymore. After that, he ran about as wild as a kid can and still stay out of jail. Don't tell me Marines aren't like that because he was, and he was a Marine, too."

"I won't try to. But what would you say if I told you that Jimmy asked me to come?"

"Favor to a dying man?"

"Put it that way if you want."

Sarah smiled. "I'd say what Jimmy said: You're a pretty good guy."

She wasn't prepared for the furious flush of embarrassment that colored Tully's face, and she watched him with a kind of pity.

He gulped his drink and then asked bluntly, "Does that help me add up?"

Sarah nodded. "Only in one column, though."

"Go ahead."

"Last night, you acted so coy, so surprised when I asked you if you were going to mine Kevin's claims. But the second thing you did when you hit town was to go have a look at them."

"You're wrong," Tully said dryly. "The second thing I did when I hit town was turn down your invitation to fight Ben Hodes."

It was Sarah's turn to blush, but she said stubbornly, "All right, the third thing, then. Why pretend this elaborate lack of interest in the Vicksburg Claims when you were in such a lather to look at them?"

"Look," Tully said earnestly. "If I'd been a hat designer before the war, I wouldn't have given these claims a second thought. But I'm a miner. So was Jimmy. We talked a lot about those claims. I used to kid him about being a millionaire. All right, when I come into his country and I'm close to the claims, what am I supposed to do? Sit in my hotel room with a good book?"

Sarah laughed in spite of herself. "Then you aren't interested in them?"

"If you mean, am I out to steal them or buy them or lease them, the answer is no."

"Okay. The second column adds up, too," Sarah said. She sipped at her drink; they were regarding each other almost warily, and Sarah, feeling a sudden guilt at cross-examining him, rose and made an unnecessary trip to look at the roast.

When she returned to her seat, Tully said, "Mind if I hold the pistol now? I want to ask you some questions."

"Go ahead."

"Alec told me Hodes had made an offer—a low offer on those claims. He said Kevin turned it down." He paused. "Could it be you're fighting off the rabble until your favorite character can starve Kevin into accepting his offer?"

A quick anger came to Sarah and then died. "That's a low blow, chum."

"Not the first one this morning though."

A knock on the door interrupted them, and Sarah left the kitchen to answer it. Tully felt a momentary irritation at this intrusion. He had satisfied her curiosity about him, and had been on the verge of satisfying his own about her relationship with Hodes. Now, it would have to wait, he supposed.

He heard the deep rumble of a man's voice and Sarah's easy answering laughter. Rising, he went down the passageway into the living room. Sarah was helping a balding, middle-aged man a couple of inches shorter than herself out of his dripping raincoat. It was the man Beth Hodes had been talking to in the bar last night.

Sarah said, "Tully, this is Sam Horne. He runs the newspaper. Tully Gibbs, Sam."

Behind his horn-rimmed glasses Horne's dark eyes were shrewd and impersonal. For a reason Tully could not have explained, he guessed immediately that Sam Horne was city bred and trained, one of the legion of those newspaper men who worked for the big dailies or press services only so long as it took them to make a stake and buy a rural newspaper of their own. His gray suit was neatly pressed, but his dark tie was askew under his button-down collar, as if proclaiming that a crease in his trousers were concession enough to the Sunday's amenities.

He held out a stubby hand and said in a surprisingly bass voice, "You must be the fellow who put Hodes through the wringer last night."

"That's supposed to be a secret, Sam," Sarah said.

Horne looked at her with a detached amusement. "I watched it myself from the club rooms upstairs, along with ten other guys." He glanced briefly at Tully. "That was strictly a once-over-lightly. Why didn't you boot him in the head when you had him down?"

Tully grinned, beginning to like Sam Horne. "That wouldn't have been proper."

Horne shook his head. "No, but it would have been simple justice."

Tully glanced at Sarah to see how she was taking this. She was laughing silently at Horne. Now she said, "Want a martini, Sam?"

Sam grimaced, "Good God, what a barbaric custom! Yes, of course I do."

Sarah disappeared into the kitchen and Horne walked into the middle of the living room, rubbing his hands and looking about him with obvious pleasure. "You know, this is what I need for my crib—a touch of the female," he said approvingly. "I've got twice the space they have and I spend twice the dough on it. Still, it always looks as if they just shot a cowboy movie in it an hour ago."

"I know what you mean," Tully said.

Horne sank into the nearest easy chair and said, "You were Jimmy's pilot, weren't you?"

Tully nodded.

"Nasty little bastard, wasn't he?" Horne observed. Tully shrugged noncommittally, as Sarah came in with the tray of martinis.

"I was just observing to your friend that Jimmy Russel, in spite of his hero's death, was a scab on the face of the body politic," Horne said pleasantly. "I can't imagine why Gibbs is back here, except to see what type of manure nourished that maggot."

"Now, Sam," Sarah said.

"Okay," Horne said. He accepted his martini and studied it critically. "For these good things we thank thee, oh Lord," he intoned, and then lifted his glass and nodded to both Tully and Sarah. "Cheers."

The talk soon turned to the war and Tully felt the dry, probing curiosity of the man. Tully was defensively trying to answer Horne's questions as to why the Navy was reluctant to put up its jets against the MIG 15's, when they heard quick footsteps ascending the stairs outside.

"That's Ma," Sarah said.

The door opened and Mrs. Moffit stepped into the room, leaving the door open behind her.

"Hi, lady," Sam said, rising. "We're gassing up without you." Mrs. Moffit came across the room and Tully saw that she was a handsome woman. Her transparent raincoat did not hide her trim figure, and there was a high color in her cheeks put there, Tully supposed, by the chill of this rainy day.

"This is Tully Gibbs, Ma," Sarah said. "My mother, Tully."

Mrs. Moffit looked politely puzzled as she extended her hand.

"I'll catch you up on him later, Ma. Want a martini?"

"Heavens, no," Mrs. Moffit said. "Why are you drinking them at this hour?"

"What's the matter with the hour?" Sam Horne demanded. "In Hollywood this would be called a late start."

"Well, get something ready for Kevin," Mrs. Moffit said. "I passed him on the stairs."

Tully glanced at Sarah and asked, "Couldn't I help him?"

Sarah shook her head promptly. "It takes him just seven minutes to climb them and he gets furious if you offer to help him," she said.

Mrs. Moffit hung up her coat and went on to the kitchen, calling over her shoulder to Sarah to set the table.

Sam Horne was watching the opened door, and from it came the sound of slow and labored shuffles. Sam glanced at his watch and then murmured, "Never underestimate the power of a Sunday dinner. Do you suppose she left the door open so the smell of that roast would hurry him up?"

Presently, old Kevin hove into sight in the doorway. Sarah, at the dining end of the big room, left off the table setting to greet him.

"Hi, old-timer," she said, and extended her hand.

Old Kevin looked scrubbed and burnished in his blue suit. His sparse white hair was neatly combed over his pink scalp, and his shave was so recent and so close that it was almost painful to behold.

He came slowly into the room, ceremoniously shook hands with Tully and then with Sam Horne who said, "Mr. Russel, I have in my hand an alcoholic concoction known as a martini. Are you too young to start acquiring a taste for them?"

Old Kevin said surprisingly, "Not if they're very very dry, Mr. Horne."

After that, Tully was content to listen. He helped Sarah get dinner on the table and by the time they sat down to it, he felt as if he had always known these easygoing and friendly people. Mrs. Moffit was anything but an aging woolly-headed female. Prodded by Sam Horne's questions, she and old Kevin started reminiscing about Azurite's boom days.

Tully was puzzled that Mrs. Moffit seemed to recall accurately events that must have happened more than sixty years ago, but slowly he began to understand that she was a storehouse of the local folklore and that, as if by osmosis, she had acquired enough of Azurite's history to gently correct old Kevin who was thirty years her senior. Inevitably, the talk was about mining and miners. Tully, his dinner finished, was listening in pleasant lethargy when Sam Horne addressed him. "What did you think of the Vicksburg Claims?"

Tully could not quite hide the surprise he felt at Horne's knowledge of his visit. He looked almost guiltily at Kevin, and then knew immediately that Kevin had probably heard all about it from Alec.

Tully addressed himself to old Kevin. "It looked to me like a mighty good prospect, Mr. Russel."

Old Kevin nodded, and Tully observed that Sarah was watching him closely. *Easy does it,* he thought, and said no more.

"Think a big outfit like Anaconda would be interested?" old Kevin asked.

Tully thought a moment and then shrugged. "That's hard to say, Mr. Russel, on what I've seen, but I doubt it. These big outfits are looking for a mountain of ore that would feed a thousand-ton mill. I can't be sure, but I don't think you have that much."

"Then it's a small operation," Sam Horne said.

Tully nodded. "Compared to what they do, yes."

While he was talking, Tully noticed old Kevin fumbling around on the inside pockets of his coat. Presently, he brought out a couple of letters and laid them on the table-cloth before him, then he reached up to the breast pocket of his coat, brought out a pair of steel-rimmed glasses and carefully put them on. By the time he was finished, he had an audience grown silent with curiosity.

Deliberately he took a letter from its envelope, held it before him and then looked around the group. "I have something to say, but I want to read this first," old Kevin said. "This is a letter I got from Jimmy a month or so before he died."

Tully's face seemed to turn to stone. Even at this distance he could recognize his own handwriting. He was aware of Sarah covertly watching him, and he knew that if his expression betrayed him now he was lost. He took a drink of water, leaned back in his chair, put his arm over its back and pulled idly at the lobe of his ear, hoping he was a picture of a man well fed and not quite bored.

Old Kevin said, "Here's what Jimmy wrote." And he began to read " 'You remember I wrote you my lieutenant is a hard-rock miner. I wish I could bring him home with me and show him Vicksburg. I don't suppose he'd be interested in it after the war because he's got a good job waiting for him. But, Dad, we could make him rich and us rich, and making him rich is the least I could do.' "

Tully did not need to feign embarrassment; he could feel the hot blush mount in his neck, and for a miserable moment he had to accept the pleased but unsurprised attention of everyone at the table.

When old Kevin ceased reading, Tully raised his hand in protest. "That's enough, Mr. Russel. I—" He faltered for lack of anything to say.

Old Kevin put the letter down, then deliberately took off his glasses, pocketed them and then leaned back in his chair. "There it is, son," he announced. "That's what I was going to say. Funny it should happen the way it has."

Tully's heart began to beat faster. To cover his excitement, he scowled and looked at old Kevin in a puzzled fashion, then he glanced at Sam Horne as if wordlessly asking for clarification.

Horne said, "It looks like you're tapped, boy."

"For what?"

Old Kevin said, "You think there's enough ore there to bother with, son?"

"To bother with?" Tully echoed. "I think there's a small fortune in it."

"Want to mine it share and share alike?"

Right on a platter, lettuce and all, Tully thought exultantly. How should he act—grateful, bewildered, thunderstruck or just plain happy? he wondered. He settled on bewilderment, looking long at old Kevin, trying to project a convincing incredulity. "Why—I'd think it would be wonderful, Mr. Russel, but I don't see where I belong in this."

Sam Horne put it bluntly, "You belong there because he wants you there. Don't go coy on us."

Tully managed an embarrassed laugh, and only afterwards dared look at Sarah. The expression of deep pleasure in her face told him that his play-acting had been convincing, and for the briefest moment he felt a sharp hangdog guilt.

"Maybe I'm not doing you any favor," old Kevin said slowly. "I don't have to tell you, I'm broke."

Tully thought of many things at once then—of the fifteen hundred dollars combat pay he had in the bank, of the ten-thousand-dollar loan he had fought Ben Hodes for last night, of the gray body of lead, zinc and silver lying up on the Vicksburg Claims and, lastly, of the steady flow of substantial checks from the smelter. He knew this was not the moment to discuss the financing; it was the moment to accept his good fortune and to secure it. He said, "I don't think that has to worry you, Mr. Russel. I could borrow enough to get a start." Then he shook his head, as if in puzzlement. "Mr. Russel, are you sure you want to do this? Are you even sure what you are doing?"

"They're his claims, aren't they?" Sam Horne asked.

Tully only nodded, watching Kevin.

The old man only said, "I'm sure."

It remained for Mrs. Moffit to express what they all seemed to feel. "I wish we had a bottle of champagne to celebrate with, don't you, Sarah?"

When Tully looked at Sarah she smiled, then she reached out with her left hand for Kevin's arm and with her right for Tully's, observing, "A handshake feels a lot better the next morning, Ma."

Smilingly, Tully and old Kevin shook hands across the table.

For two hours the four of them talked, making plans, spending money they did not have and then laughing at themselves. Old Kevin revealed then that the smelter reports on his tests had shown fourteen per cent lead, twenty-eight ounces silver and seventeen per cent zinc, confirming the figures Jimmy had told Tully.

They all agreed that the greatest expense would be in constructing the road which properly deserved the financial aid of the county. Old Kevin, through the years, had obtained easements for a road through other properties, so there would be no trouble on that score. Horne explained, in his wry way, what Tully had already learned from Alec, that the county commissioners stubbornly refused Kevin any road aid.

"Still, I'd like to talk to them," Tully said finally. "When do they meet?"

Sarah and Horne looked at each other, and then Sam said, "Why, tomorrow, isn't it, Sarah?" It was agreed then that Tully would appear before them for one more try. And then their conversation returned to the claims. Discounting the windfall of a new road, it was Kevin's idea, and Tully concurred, that once a road was in, a winter's mining of high-grade ore would make the purchase of a small mill possible, and once they were able to ship concentrates, the real expansion would come.

In the late afternoon Sam Horne had to leave and only

then did the women, with Tully's help, stir themselves to clear off the table and clean up.

When Sarah and Tully returned to the living room, old Kevin was sleeping soundly in the most comfortable chair, a slight wispy little man whose sleep was as deep and dreamless as a child's.

Tully halted and looked down at Kevin and presently he heard Sarah stir beside him.

"I've got something to tell my kids," Tully murmured. "It's not true that Santa Claus has a beard."

"Maybe Kevin has just discovered that too," Sarah said. "You see, he counted on Jimmy for so long, but Jimmy wouldn't help him. Jimmy couldn't be bothered as long as there was a crap game floating around. I guess crap games are what decided Jimmy. The sports around town took him. He owed so much he had to leave town for a while. I guess that started him thinking, and he realized that the Vicksburg Claims were his only shortcut to money, real money. But by that time it was too late; the draft was breathing down his neck." She shrugged. "Then Kevin counted on the government and they turned him down. All he had left was Ben Hodes and his offer of a one and a half per cent interest. So maybe you're Santa Claus too, Tully."

Oddly, Tully felt a relief at her words. They made his letters of self-praise, his scheming and even his greed seem less reprehensible after all. It didn't matter how he achieved his partnership so long as it was his money and his work that would develop it. Yet, the guilt lingered and he knew he was deceiving himself.

It was time to go and when Mrs. Moffit returned to the room, Tully rose, thanked them for the dinner and excused himself. He shook hands with Sarah last and, his hand on the doorknob, he paused and looked down at her. "I can't help but think you had something to do with all this," he said.

Sarah nodded. "You don't think we'd turn old Kevin loose with just anyone, do you? You may not know it, but

you were right up on the meat block this afternoon, like the
new beau meeting the girl's family."

Tully grinned. "I'm in, then?"

"Like Flynn," Sarah said.

3

Ben Hodes came in from the back porch and tramped through the dark kitchen into the library and dumped the load of wood he carried with a great crash into the metal wood basket. He hoped the racket would waken his sister, Beth, who was resting upstairs; he was lonely and wanted company.

His Sunday had been a glum one. He had been unable to get hold of Sarah to explain his leave-taking last night. She would be at old Kevin Russel's, he supposed, and would resent his coming there. He could, of course, have killed the day at the Elks Club shooting billiards or playing cards, as was the custom on a rainy Sunday evening, but each time he thought of it he remembered his face. His lip was cut and swollen, but it would be down enough by tomorrow so that it would not disfigure him. The scratches on his cheek from the cinders were barely noticeable, yet these marks loomed enormously in his mind as a visible token of his defeat.

Stoking the fire in the pleasant, tall windowed living room, he stood before the fireplace a moment, big hands on his hips. He wore an oversized sweat shirt that made his upper body huge and almost formless. Almost gently he touched his ribs and winced. He had taken a genuine beating, he knew, and oddly enough there was little resentment in him. He had picked on the wrong man and, what was worse, had pegged him for a coward because of his refusal to fight in the hotel bar. He'd thought Gibbs's yarn about the broken legs was just crawling, whereas it was true. He'd simply guessed wrong. It was that simple. Yet how was he to know that the man who refused him a fight in the afternoon would lick him at night?

Restlessly he cruised around the heavy furniture and finally hauled up in front of the cabinet bar. Here he poured himself a shot of whiskey, moved across to the big leather chair by the fire and was slacking into it when the bell pull sounded.

Swearing softly, he set his drink on the mantelpiece and went out of the room into the corridor to answer the door. For the thousandth time he cursed the frosted glass pane of the door which did not allow identification of a caller and made every visitor to the house a stranger until the door was opened.

Palming open the door, he stood silent in disbelief, without giving greeting. His visitor was Tully Gibbs. Ben's hand started to move to touch his lip and then fell to his side.

Gibbs said, "I'd like to see you, if you aren't busy."

Ben stood undecided and then, too proud to show unease, he swung the door open and said surlily, "Come inside."

He led the way into the library, indicated the other easy chair opposite his own, and said, "Want a drink?"

Tully said he did. Ben named his stock, Tully made his choice and as Ben mixed the drink, he covertly regarded his visitor. There was a sort of "go-to-hell" look on Gibbs's lean face even when relaxed, and Ben found himself more curious about the man than resentful.

He handed Gibbs his drink, picked up his own, and sank into the chair. Then he lifted his glass and said with a wry humor, "Here's to back-alley fighting."

Gibbs said nothing, only grinned faintly, but without derision.

"I'd like a return engagement sometime," Ben said.

Gibbs looked at him obliquely, sardonically. "The footing isn't so good this afternoon, but if you insist . . ."

He left his invitation hanging and Ben laughed suddenly.

"Good God, man, give me time for my bruises to turn green."

Gibbs didn't smile this time and Ben regarded him curiously. His lean face seemed strained and overlaid with a kind of tension that was foreign to Ben. He was, Hodes thought grudgingly, not exactly handsome and certainly not homely, but there was an engaging directness about him that was undeniable.

Ben wondered what he wanted and thought, *I'll let him fry*. However, after a minute's silence, it was Ben who was the more uncomfortable. Gibbs sat staring into the fire occasionally sipping his drink, utterly content with the quiet of the room.

Ben leaned forward. "Look, if you've come to crow, get it out of your system."

Gibbs looked closely at him and said, "You don't remember, then?"

Ben scowled. "Remember what?"

"Our bet?"

Ben's scowl deepened. He cast memory back over last evening for the dozenth time and now something new served as a prod. He'd been pretty well loaded, he recalled. The mention of a bet seemed to focus memory. Of course there had been a bet, he recalled distinctly. But what was it? He said aggressively, "Of course I remember. You were to leave Sarah alone if I licked you."

"And you didn't," Gibbs pointed out.

Ben laughed. "All right, you don't have to leave her alone."

Gibbs looked sharply at him. "Is this the beginning of a welsh?"

Ben's anger was immediate. "If you're looking for a hassle right in this room, that's the way to get it." He pushed his pride aside. "What was the bet, then?"

"Your signature on a ten-thousand-dollar, hundred-and-twenty-day note at your bank."

Ben slowly sat back in his chair digesting this bit of information. Now that it was recalled to him, he remembered it.

But why did he ever make the bet, he wondered. He asked Tully, "What did you put up?"

Gibbs said sardonically, "You seemed so anxious for me to stay away from Miss Moffit that that was all I had to put up—my promise that I'd let her alone if I lost."

Ben flushed. "Come to collect?"

"That's the general idea."

Ben finished his drink and then asked abruptly, "That's an odd way to get a bank loan. What's the dough for?"

"That's my business," Gibbs answered coldly.

Ben shrugged and stood up. "All right, I'll call the bank tomorrow and tell them to let you have it."

"I'd just as soon you'd call them now."

"Are you still afraid of my welshing?"

Gibbs looked at him carefully. "Yes."

The insolence of his reply brought a swift anger to Ben and a moment later a kind of wry appreciation of Gibbs's gall. Momentarily, he wished he knew more about the man —why he was here and how long he would stay. Sarah and the boys around town had told him only that Gibbs was Jimmy Russel's pilot and had been shot down along with Jimmy.

He rose now and said amiably, "If I go on your note, it's elementary common sense to ask you how you expect to pay me back."

"Either you make a bet and keep it, or you don't," Gibbs said. "What'll it be?" He got up too.

They eyed each other warily for a long moment and then Ben moved over to the phone by the table in front of the window. He called Harry Bogue's house and instructed him to give Gibbs a certified check for ten thousand dollars tomorrow morning. He further instructed him to draw up a one-hundred-and-twenty-day note for that sum for Tully to sign. At Bogue's murmur of protest, Ben slammed down the receiver, turned and said, "That satisfy you?"

Gibbs nodded, moved across the room to set his glass on the bar top and said, "Thanks very much."

"You're not going to see Sarah any more, you know," Ben said easily.

"Want to make a bet on that, too?" Gibbs retorted.

Ben shook his head and smiled. "Nope, I just know it."

He moved out into the hall and let Gibbs out and neither said goodbye.

When Ben turned away from the door he saw Beth standing motionless on the stairs. He halted, and they looked at each other a silent moment.

"How much of that did you hear?"

"Almost all of it," Beth said softly. She came down the stairs and turned into the living room. She was wearing a denim skirt and red checked blouse, and as she crossed the room she ran her hand through her dark unruly hair. It was a gesture of his mother's, Ben remembered, and for a moment he felt fierce and overwhelming protectiveness for his sisters.

Beth took a cigarette from a box on the coffee table, lighted it, and then stood with her back to the fire. She eyed Ben closely as he tramped across the room and slacked into one of the leather chairs facing the fireplace. Her face, broad at the cheekbones, held a sort of resigned serenity at the moment. In repose and not animated as in conversation, it held an almost sad maturity. Now it was possible to believe that she was two years Ben's senior and truly his older sister.

Ben said sullenly, "Go ahead."

"All right. Who is he?"

"The guy that licked me last night."

"I know that."

"Then why'd you ask?"

Beth said tranquilly, "Because you loaned him money. On what collateral, may I ask, and why, since you must hate his liver and lights?"

Ben leaned back and crossed his legs. "Don't play the heavy banker, sis."

"It's as much my money as yours."

"You tried to prove that once and got tossed off the Board of Directors for a while, remember?"

Beth flushed and said nothing.

"What are you going to do about it?"

"The same as usual. Nothing."

At her reply Ben smiled. "That's right. And since you won't I see no reason to go into it."

Beth watched him a moment and then said dryly, "You're a lovable cuss, little brother. Sometimes I wonder why you've been allowed to live as long as you have." She spoke without passion or anger. It was as if their basic conflicts, vitiated by a thousand scenes, had become only a formality of calm name-calling. All the anger was long since washed out and it was routine.

"Thank you, my dear," Ben murmured. He regarded her carefully now. "You aren't getting any ideas, are you?"

"About what?"

"That Gibbs."

Beth eyed Ben a long moment, and a faint humor crept into her dark eyes. "I'd love to hire you out for a toad."

"Because if you are," Ben said flatly, "get it out of your head. Remember Frank Nichols."

"Oh, but Gibbs doesn't work for you. You can't fire him like you did Frank just for calling on me." She paused, and unable to resist the impulse, she said, "You can't even lick him."

"I can see that he's licked," Ben said levelly.

Beth stared at him a long moment. "I believe you would. Only you have nothing to worry about. I'm too well trained to look at a man." She continued with a certain grimness in her levity. "I haven't thanked you for letting me out to go to the dance last night. I enjoyed talking with the ladies, and I didn't speak to more than two men under sixty-five."

"That's two too many," Ben said. "Next time, don't."

"Yes, master," Beth said with a mock meekness that did not quite come off. "Let's fight about something else."

"I meant what I said," Ben said flatly. "Don't get any

ideas about Gibbs. I'm already fighting him off my girl. Damned if I want to fight him off my sister."

Beth turned and threw her cigarette in the fire. "If you're through with my Sunday scolding, I think I'll go up and bathe."

Ben moved toward the bar, wanting a drink. At that moment the doorbell jangled softly. Ben looked over at Beth and growled. "You'd think this damn house was a railroad station."

Beth, who was closest, moved through the living room into the hall and opened the door. Sam Horne stood there, hat in hand, an almost sheepish smile on his face. "I believe we were interrupted in a conversation last night," Sam said, then added, grinning, "That's a lousy way to say I'd like to see you again."

For a moment Beth hesitated. She knew her smile was artificial, and that she was already afraid of what Ben would do. Then the recklessness of desperation came to her. "Then come in, Sam."

She stepped aside, and Sam entered the hall, shucking off his coat and handing it and his hat to Beth. Beth put them on the hall-tree and fearfully led the way into the living room.

Ben, standing by the portable bar, a fresh drink in his hand, was glaring at Sam as Beth said, with only a small quaver in her voice, "Sam, you know my brother, Ben, of course."

Sam nodded. Ben said nothing, only glared as Sam moved over to the big sofa in front of the fire.

"Like a drink?" Beth asked. She had not looked at Ben yet but she could almost feel the tension building up in the room. She knew what was coming, what always came when a man called on her.

"I don't think it would cripple me. Bourbon, please, if you have it."

Beth moved over to the bar which Ben was blocking. She said, "Excuse me, Ben," and looked fleetingly into his face. The sullenness which was never entirely absent from Ben's face was plain now. He took a grudging step aside, and Beth began to mix two drinks.

Sam said, conversationally, "What did Notre Dame do yesterday?"

"I don't follow them," Ben said curtly.

There was an awkward silence, during which the sound of Beth's drink-mixing was the only thing that could be heard in the room.

Desperately now, Beth returned with Sam's drink and handed it to him. Her hand was shaking so that the ice tinkled in the glass. Sam, noting it, grinned and observed, "You must have had a big night."

Beth smiled shyly at him. "No. Ben brought me home early."

"She's always home early," Ben said heavily. "I see to that."

Sam glanced over at him. "You don't approve of late hours?"

"No."

"Except for yourself, you mean?"

"I don't approve of late hours for Beth," Ben said.

Sam gazed speculatively at Ben for a moment, and then shifted his glance to Beth. "I've always known your brother as a mining man, but never as a house mother," he observed.

His jibe stirred Ben into movement, and Beth thought miserably, *Please, Sam, be quiet.*

Ben tramped over to stand beside Beth, his back to the fire. He said now, with total boorishness, "Why are you here, may I ask?"

Sam regarded him coldly. "I had the impression I was going to call on your sister."

"She doesn't like callers," Ben said flatly.

Sam raised his eyebrows and said, "Oh?" and Beth caught the question in his eye as he looked at her.

"That's not true, Ben!" she said warmly. And then, to cover up her brother's rudeness she said, "You had too much to drink last night and you're grouchy. Why don't you go up and take a nap?"

"I'll stay here."

Beth knew she was defeated, and that something dismally unpleasant was going to happen. This was confirmed by the look of mockery in Sam Horne's eyes. "Can you think of any pleasant three-cornered conversation?" Sam asked.

"No," Ben said bluntly.

"Canasta, maybe," Sam went on. "It's cold outside and this whiskey's good."

Beth pounced on Sam's suggestion. "That's a good idea, Sam. I'll get the card table."

"No, you won't," Ben said flatly.

Beth had started to move. Now she halted obediently, and looked desperately at Sam.

"Maybe I could get it," Sam said easily.

"You won't get it either."

Sam sighed and stood up.

"Well, they say every man's home is his castle, and brother, you've certainly made a dungeon out of this one."

Alarm came to Beth, and she said, "Sam, please don't."

"I know what you're thinking," Sam said. "The big lug will swing on me." His glance shuttled to Ben. "I don't think he will. Some prep-school master a long time ago told him that gentlemen don't do that to guests in their home. He thinks he's a gentleman."

"Please, Sam!"

"Let him talk," Ben said solemnly. "After he's through, he can leave."

Sam set his glass down on the end table. "With your permission I'll just do that. Hodes, just what are your plans for Beth?"

Ben scowled. "What do you mean by that?"

"I mean, she hasn't any plans for herself. You must have some for her."

"Are any plans necessary?"

"Not always, but they help. For instance, you could say that a good third of the guys in Sing Sing have no definite plans. Most people do though, for their families—even their sister."

Ben said sullenly, "That's no concern of yours."

"No, I'm very concerned about what'll happen to a nice girl. You haven't got to the stage of a chastity belt and hiding her shoes yet, but you're warming up."

Beth listened to this interchange with increasing despair. She could see that Sam Horne was angry and that his anger, oddly enough, was beginning to amuse Ben. Her brother's total arrogance and total confidence went beyond swinishness. It was as if he knew that he could not help but win in the end, and that those pinpricks were not even bothersome.

Ben observed now, "You've got quite a lip for a Sunday afternoon caller."

Beth saw that Sam was ignoring Ben now; he was looking at her with an open pity in his dark eyes.

"I'm sorry about this, Beth. You always seemed to me a pleasant, lonesome girl. I wish I could help."

His glance shuttled to Ben. "May I say that in my time I have been a loving collector of SOB's, but you, my friend, are a cabinet piece. It's my fondest wish that Beth present you with an illegitimate nephew."

To Beth he said, "I hope you understand. Goodbye."

Belatedly, Beth followed him, but Sam left the room, snatched up his coat and hat and let himself out. When she saw she was too late, she halted, then turned and looked at Ben.

"I'll never forgive you for that, Ben! Never!"

"If I've told you once, I've told you a thousand times, I don't want men hanging around you."

"But what am I supposed to do!" Beth cried passionately. "Live out my life like a nun?"

"The men in this town are trash. You're too good for them."

"Then find me a good man!"

"He'll come along."

"How will I ever meet him? You'd insult him and order him out of the house!"

She came over to him now and halted before him. Her anger was dead, and all she felt was the naked need to tell Ben.

"Ben, please, please!" she begged. "Give me back my life! I can't live like this. I'm not meant to! Nobody's meant to! I'm an old maid. I've only been kissed once in my life. Is that what a woman's supposed to be?"

"You're getting hysterical. You're attractive, and someday the right man will come along. Until then—"

"I know," Beth said bitterly, "I mustn't be friendly with any man who hasn't gray hair."

Suddenly she struck out at Ben. Effortlessly, Ben put out his hand, caught her wrist before her palm could touch his face and held it with a great gentleness.

Beth wrenched free and ran out of the room.

When Tully was finished shaving Monday morning, he was faced with a mild dilemma. Should he impress the commissioners as a solid mining engineer with big-city backing by wearing his pin-stripe suit, or would they be less suspicious of him if he came before them in the careless clothes of a working miner? He chose the suit, dressed carefully, had a late, leisurely breakfast and was standing on the red sandstone steps of the Grant County Bank when it was opened at ten o'clock by a harried-looking middle-aged man whose rimless glasses added to the normal chill of his gray eyes.

This was Mr. Harry Bogue, and his disapproval of Tully was massive. He let himself into his office and soon appeared behind the wicket with the cashier's check. He proffered it and the note in silence and Tully accepted the check and signed the note in the same manner. They nodded coldly to each other, and then Tully stepped out, heading downstreet for the courthouse and the commissioners' meeting.

The commissioners' room was on the first floor, a high-ceilinged, spacious room holding a long table. The walls were lined with chairs, some of which were occupied by petitioners like himself. Three men sat at the big table in old-fashioned swivel chairs and Sarah, as the clerk's deputy, was just finishing reading the minutes of the last meeting as Tully slipped into the chair nearest the door.

Sarah was wearing an orange wool dress—probably, Tully thought, out of protest against the dun-colored walls and the drab countrymen's clothes of the commissioners. The wicker bottom of the chair creaked as Tully eased into it. Sarah looked up and for one astonished moment, beholding Tully in his business suit, she looked only surprised, then she smiled her greeting and returned to the reading of the minutes.

Tully had a chance to study the three commissioners and, remembering Sam Horne's description of them, he identified the slight, wiry man in denim pants and jumper at the head of the table as Bill Wishnack, their chairman. Wishnack's lean, weather-burned face contrasted sharply with the pale skin of his forehead and his almost bald head which was crossed from ear to ear by a thinning saddle of jet-black hair. He was bored and impatient and kept glancing at Tully with a covert suspicion, as if wondering why anyone would wear a suit unless he were attending a funeral.

When Sarah finished reading the minutes, Wishnack moved that they be approved and then settled back in his swivel chair. He pointed a callused finger at one of the men seated against the wall and asked courteously, "Who's first?"

A man in bib overalls rose, came to the table and seated himself, and he was already talking. It seemed he wanted a culvert placed in the road several hundred yards below his farm because his neighbor's runaway irrigation left the road a perpetual mire.

Tully listened attentively. The petitioner was addressing a heavyset man with a big head, topped by an uncombatable mat of short, dead gray hair. This would be Justin Byers he remembered, and he understood suddenly why these men, and especially Byers, had been commissioners almost in perpetuity. They were considerate, grave and patient, and exactly the same sort of people as those who usually petitioned them. Byers had a florid, heavily veined face with deep hound's creases graven at the corners of his mouth. His pale eyes were large and morose and when he spoke, his voice was oddly gentle. He might have been a priest listening with deep compassion to the old old sins of humanity.

The remaining commissioner, Harvey Peebles, was a long, angular, cheerful-looking rancher whose hearing was impaired and who listened with his great calloused hand cupped to his ear. Tully found Sarah the most attractive thing in the room.

The culvert was disposed of and the petitioner left. Then Bill Wishnack addressed Tully. "You wanted to see us?"

Tully moved toward the seat at the big table and Sarah said, "Gentlemen, this is Mr. Tully Gibbs, a mining engineer." Her introduction called for the shaking of hands all around.

Then Tully seated himself and began to state his case. He said that he had looked over some claims located in the county and that he had confirmed the presence of a large body of high-grade ore. He and his associates were preparing to develop the property, but before doing so he wished to know the attitude of the county toward a new industry.

Bill Wishnack said bluntly, "Why, we'd welcome it, Mr. Gibbs. We already have one crackerjack mine in this county and we'd like a dozen more on our tax rolls." He paused. "Just where is this property?"

"I'll come to that later," Tully said matter-of-factly. "I'm mostly interested in how much help you feel you could give us in opening up the property and maintaining a road to it. I already have easements for the road and I'd be willing to deed the road to the county in exchange for help."

Bill Wishnack squirmed deeper into his chair, put his elbows on the arms and steepled his fingers under his chin. "Depends on where it is, Mr. Gibbs."

"With what you'll eventually get from us in tax money, I think you could afford it even if it were on Black Mountain Peak."

The commissioners all smiled dutifully at this mild joke.

"You plan a year-round operation?" Harvey Peebles asked.

Tully nodded and Peebles looked at the others. "Shouldn't think maintaining it would be any problem," he observed.

"Wait a minute," Wishnack said slowly. "Before we make any promises, we'd better find out where your mine is."

"Vicksburg Hill," Tully said quietly. He was watching Byers's eyes, and they reminded him of a shade being pulled down over a window. Byers did not even have to look at the other two; he studied the pencil in his hand and thrust out his full lower lip in a thoughtful sort of pout.

Wishnack cleared his throat. "Those are the Russel claims, Mr. Gibbs?"

"That's right."

Wishnack straightened up. "I don't think we'll be able to give you any help on your road, Mr. Gibbs. We've been over this with Mr. Russel."

"You were pretty helpful until you learned where the claims were," Tully said sardonically, looking at Byers. "Suppose I'd said they were on Black Mountain?"

Byers lifted his morose glance and regarded Tully with suffering patience. "You don't understand, Mr. Gibbs," he said gently. "Vicksburg Hill is a long way from the closest access road. Suppose we spent ten thousand dollars putting in the road for you. What guarantee have we got that tax money from you will help pay for it?"

"Because there's ore there and a lot of it."

Wishnack said abruptly, "Suppose you show us your drill logs."

"The property has not been diamond-drilled, Mr. Wishnack. We're not Anaconda. We're simply a small mine with a good body of top-grade ore."

"You hope," Harvey Peebles said dryly.

"We know," Tully corrected him.

"We're not doubting your judgment," Byers said slowly. "Only we need more than your opinion." He leaned forward in his chair, an expression of deep earnestness on his sorrowing face. "Mr. Gibbs, here's our problem. The state allows us to spend only so much of county money for roads. Our maintenance problems here are terrible. Sometimes, in one week we have to move two three-foot snowfalls. We spend twice and three times what other countries do in just keeping our roads open. We can't afford to build new ones."

"That's a speculation not allowed us," Wishnack put in.

"But you'll build an access road to a ranch, won't you?"

"Ranches pay taxes," Harvey Peebles said.

"So do mines," Tully countered.

"Just what tax money have you paid, Mr. Gibbs?" Wishnack asked, and smiled sourly to blunt the barb of his question.

Tully glanced briefly at Sarah. Her face was masked by a pretended attentiveness, but the lack of hope was there. Tully realized bitterly that these men held Sarah's livelihood in their hands. She was a deputy paid to cooperate with them and carry out their decisions, however wrong-headed they were. He had no right to expect any help from her. The thing to do, he knew, was to swallow their refusal to help with as much grace as he could muster, at the same time driving the best possible bargain.

"I can see your point there," he said reasonably. "No reason why a latecomer on the scene should demand preferential treatment, is there?"

Byers gave a soft sigh of relief and said piously, "We try to take care of our own first, Mr. Gibbs."

Our own what? Tully thought sourly. He said, "That's understandable. Still, as a prospective heavy taxpayer, I think I may be entitled to some consideration."

"What consideration, Mr. Gibbs?" Wishnack asked carefully.

"Well, if I'm going to have to build a county road at my own expense, there are a couple of ways you could help me. For instance, I'll need a bulldozer. It would be a real break for me if I could rent it from the county for what I'd depreciate it plus a very modest rental. The same would apply for one of your four-wheel-drive trucks when it's not plowing."

Before he was finished, Wishnack was shaking his head in negation. "We'd be happy to do that, Mr. Gibbs, except it's an iron-clad rule that no county equipment can be rented out."

"No exceptions?"

"Sorry, no exceptions."

Tully felt a savage exasperation which he could not entirely hide and he said, "So I rent one in Galena for plenty of dough, is that it? Who made that iron-clad rule, Mr. Wishnack—the Board of County Commissioners?"

Wishnack nodded. "Yes—out of simple self-protection."

Tully tried another tack then. "Once I get a road in, will the county help me maintain it, always supposing I'd deed it to the county?"

Wishnack gave Byers a fleeting and wary glance, and then said, "Suppose we settle that when your road is built, Mr. Gibbs."

This then was total defeat, or almost total, Tully thought. He made one last try. "Well, gentlemen, I don't seem to be getting much in the way of positive help from Grant County. I wonder if you'd be willing to help me in a negative way."

"Explain that, Mr. Gibbs," Peebles said courteously.

"Well, when my mine is hauling out ore, it'll be taxable. It will be easy enough for you to ask the county assessor to place a low evaluation on the property until I've recovered part of the cost of building a road."

Wishnack said blandly, "The county assessor is not an appointive office in this state, Mr. Gibbs. It's elective, and he goes his own way. If you feel like appealing your assessment, we'll hear you."

That's it, Tully thought with disgust. He hadn't even succeeded in bumming a cigarette from these three sterling public servants. Rising, he shook hands all round, said courteously, "Thank you, gentlemen," and replaced his chair at the table. He gave Sarah a fleeting glance and saw that she was studiously recording the decision of the commissioners. He went out.

On Tully's exit, Sarah went into the County Clerk's office adjoining the commissioners' room and returned with a batch of warrants for the commissioners to sign. Wishnack rose and got a drink at the marble-topped sink in the corner. Justin Byers rose, too, said, "I'll be back in a minute," and stepped out into the corridor.

Turning left, he padded softly down the corridor and looked into the assessor's office. Behind the counter on which a plat book was opened, a blond girl, trim of figure and wearing a shrieking red dress, was typing.

Byers walked around the counter, saying in his soft voice, "Morning, Ann."

She smiled at him as he halted before her.

"You take a walk, honey. I've got a call to make."

Dutifully the girl rose and left the room. When Byers was certain she was out of hearing, he moved the phone on her desk toward him, dialed a number, and after again making sure that there was nobody in the hall, he turned his back upon it.

Then, he said in answer to the voice on the other end of the wire, "This is Justin. I've got to see you right away." He was silent a moment and then said, "But we're meeting this morning." He was silent another moment, then said, "All right, be right out."

He hung up the receiver, retraced his steps to the commissioners' room. Instead of seating himself, he lifted a dust-colored, narrow-brim Stetson from its wall hook and said, "I've got an appointment with the doc that I can't get out of, Bill. I'll sign those later," and he nodded toward the stack of folded vouchers and warrants on the table.

Wishnack was signing his name. Without looking up, he said, "What's the matter with you?"

"Gas," Byers said mysteriously. Nobody said anything and he went out.

Parked in front of the courthouse were a dozen cars. Byers went to the most dilapidated one, a pickup with a battered stake body and flapping fenders.

Backing out, Byers turned down Main Street, traveled its

length and, presently, where the gravel road forked, he turned left up the canyon.

The Mahaffey Mine lay two miles up New York Gulch. Its galvanized tin buildings, staggered in steps down the base of the mountain where it met the flats, were shining brightly in the midday sunlight.

Byers parked his truck alongside a dozen other cars on the parking lot, and the moment he shut off his motor he picked up the low rumble of the grinding mill in operation up the slope. As he tramped toward the office door, he wondered how people could work in the constant din of the mill, forgetting that much of his life was spent listening to the noisy roar of a working tractor.

The office he entered held behind its low counter a huge safe and filing cabinets, plus a pair of metal desks at which two middle-aged women were working.

Byers nodded to them, went through the gate at the end of the counter and hauled up at the frosted glass door marked Private. He knocked, was bidden enter, and stepped into Ben Hodes's office.

This was a sunny, comfortable room which Ben Hodes had left just as his father furnished it. It held an ancient rolltop desk, a floor-to-ceiling rack of paper-stuffed pigeonholes and a long glass case containing a variety of tagged ore samples. Against the opposite wall was a long table littered with magazines and mining journals, and on the wall above it was a panoramic view of the original Mahaffey Mine and its workings.

Hodes was seated in a swivel chair at the hulking desk, his feet hoisted to the writing board which groaned each time he moved the massive weight of his legs. He was coatless and seemed to Byers to be loafing luxuriously.

"What's up, Justin?" Hodes asked, and then grinned. "You sounded as if you'd just lost your favorite dog in the bailer."

"A dollar says that in ten minutes you'll be feeling as bad as I sounded."

Under Ben's scowl, he threw his hat on the table, swung a chair out from the wall and eased his soft bulk into it.

"Now what?" Ben asked cautiously.

"Did you know Kevin Russel is starting to mine those Vicksburg Claims?" Justin asked softly.

"Who's been ribbing you?" Hodes scoffed.

"A fellow by the name of Tully Gibbs."

At this announcement, Hodes swung his feet off the desk and settled them on the floor with a surprising gentleness. He was staring at Byers in open disbelief.

"Gibbs?" he echoed, and then hesitated. "How do you know that?"

"Gibbs came before the commissioners this morning wanting county help on a road to Vicksburg Hill."

For ten full seconds Hodes was silent, glaring at Byers, then he reached out for the phone on his desk and swiftly, with a savage intensity, dialed a number.

"Harry?" he asked then, "have you given that party his certified check?"

Upon receiving the answer, Hodes groaned softly, then he said irritably, "I know, I know. All right," and slowly replaced the receiver.

For long seconds he stared at the wall ahead of him, then slowly turned his big head. "What a chump," he murmured.

"Who? Gibbs?"

"A-ah, never mind," Hodes said bitterly. Lifting his hand, he scrubbed his mouth savagely, and then winced when the pressure touched his torn lip. Rising then, he shot the swivel chair back until it crashed against the table. Ramming both hands in his hip pockets, he moved over to the window and looked out at the sun-drenched reaches of far New York Gulch.

He said then, over his shoulder, "What did you tell him?"

"Gibbs? Why, to go to hell, of course," Byers said, a tone of injury creeping into his soft voice. "Bill gave him a pretty thorough runaround. First, he wanted us to build him a road, then he wanted to rent our equipment, and then he wanted his taxes excused." Byers hesitated. "He's serious, Ben."

"Don't I damn well know it," Hodes said angrily, and turned back to the window again.

Presently he wheeled and slowly walked back to his chair which he dragged up to the desk with the vehemence of suppressed wrath. The whole clever scheme of Gibbs's was apparent to him now. He had lost not only his last opportunity to force old Kevin into giving up the Vicksburg Claims, but he, and he alone, had been instrumental in financing his own defeat. There was no doubt in his mind that the ten-thousand-dollar loan the bank made Gibbs would go toward working the claims. Gibbs had been clever as hell, Ben thought. He had parlayed a simple pickup of Sarah into working capital for his mine.

Ben sat down and grimly regarded his desk blotter. He knew all too well how Gibbs would operate. The bulk of his loan would be spent on constructing a road to the claims. By the time it was in operation, his miners would have the highest-grade ore in the bin and waiting for the trucks. The custom mill over at Galena was a short haul. In a hundred and twenty days Gibbs would have his loan repaid, his road built and a sweet little mine working around the clock. In another year, he would have a mill of his own. Old Kevin Russel would be drinking seven-dollar-a-bottle whiskey and Gibbs would have a new convertible.

Ben said grimly, "He's got to be stopped."

Byers chuckled appreciatively. "That'll take some doing."

Ben rose again and slowly tramped back to the window, a wild restlessness pushing him. He cast about in his mind for Gibbs's vulnerable points, considering them carefully. Finally, he said over his shoulder, "What'll he do for machinery?"

"He said he'd have to rent the stuff from Galena."

That would be the Uinta Construction Company, Ben supposed. Well, he had the money to rent it now, he thought savagely.

He half turned back to Byers. "Know who'll work for him?"

"Old man Russel knows every miner in this country. That won't be hard."

That was true, Ben thought sourly. Gibbs had the money and the technical know-how, while old Kevin could certainly come up with practical advice.

Hodes turned his head and stared morosely out at the distant mountains. Up to now a case of whiskey at Christmas for each commissioner had been enough to keep them friendly toward him and cooperative, since their own selfish interests coincided with his. As the county's major taxpayer, they were understandably anxious to please him. Byers's presence here was testimony to that. Yet, in his emergency, he thought wryly, they were powerless to help him.

Or were they?

Impulsively he turned to examine Byers coldly, as if he were first seeing the man. He was remembering all he knew of him. Byers had some poor land, and a few head of cattle up Officer's Creek way. He was lazy, a born gossip, and was enormously proud of his commissioner's job. To retain it he faithfully neglected his ranch and just as faithfully did the bidding of the group of hidebound, conservative ranchers to which he fancied he belonged.

Ben asked bluntly, "Is there any legal way you commissioners can stop Gibbs?"

Byers pondered a moment. "I don't see how."

Ben bulled ahead. "It's worth ten thousand dollars to me to find a way." He walked slowly over to his chair, sat down, and only then looked at Byers.

Byers's glance was veiled. He said in agreement, "If you figure to pick up those claims someday, I'd judge it's worth that to you."

Ben smiled faintly. "You don't get it, Justin. I said—"

"I heard you," Byers cut in softly and his eyes were suddenly sharp. "Every act of the Board of Commissioners is known to the people. We're watched. What you need is a good lawyer, Ben."

"I don't think so," Hodes said softly. "If my money's going out, I want it to go to my friends."

"Sometimes friends can't accept it without the whole world knowing it," Byers observed.

He's got it, Ben thought, and he said, "There are lots of ways to arrange that without it ever showing."

Byers straightened up in his chair and once again his eyes were veiled. "You'd like me to pass around this information?" Byers asked carefully.

Hodes shook his head emphatically. "I would not. I'll deny I ever said it if you repeat it. But the offer stands."

Byers rose. So did Hodes. Ben stepped over, held out his hand. "Thanks for the visit, Justin."

Byers shook hands with him and they looked at each other steadily, with mutual understanding.

"No trouble at all, no trouble at all."

4

It was Sarah's idea that out of consideration for Kevin's physical infirmities they should meet at his house that evening. And it was several minutes after seven o'clock, the appointed time, when Tully knocked on the door. When Sarah opened it, Tully could hear immediately the low rumble of Sam Horne's voice and the higher-pitched and softer tones of Alec answering him.

Tully said, "Sorry I'm late, Sarah. After the third time I fell on my face, I went back to buy a flashlight."

Sarah smiled, saying, "It doesn't matter." Tully walked past her into the shabby linoleum-floored living room. The voices, Tully saw, were all coming from the kitchen. Turning to Sarah, he asked quietly, "Still speaking to me after that sorry job I did this morning?"

"What was sorry about it? The whole thing was loaded and you knew it."

Tully shook his head. "I didn't look good."

"You didn't lose your temper anyway."

"That's the only thing I didn't lose."

"Let's forget it," Sarah said. "It was a very dignified hassle and you lost it." She started toward the kitchen and Tully fell in behind her.

Kevin, Sam Horne and Alec Bacchione were seated at the big round oilcloth-covered kitchen table. With its clustered chairs, the table took up all the space in the tiny kitchen that was not occupied by the big, black iron coal range and the rusty sink.

When Sam Horne saw Tully, he said jeeringly, "Hail the conquered hero. Brush the dust off your knees. You don't need to kneel to us."

Tully only grinned and said hello to Kevin and Alec. Then he seated Sarah and slipped into a chair between her and Alec, who said, "Has the mining consultant come to confer with his associates?"

Sarah laughed. "He almost had them fooled, Alec, so don't tease him. He sounded very important."

"He is important," old Kevin said.

"Don't build him up, Pop," Sam Horne said. "He looks too much like a young executive right now."

"It's the suit," Tully said. "I promise never to do it again."

Sam Horne touched a match to his cigarette and then said in mock soberness, "Mr. Gibbs, the *Nugget*'s Market Edition will hit the street in four days. Anaconda has kept a wire open from Butte since ten o'clock this morning. They all want to know what the syndicate plans for Vicksburg. Have you any statements that you care to give me to throw away?"

Tully grinned. "Sure. The syndicate is starting work tomorrow."

"My God, I'd better sell my Phelps-Dodge," Horne said.

Sarah said seriously, "Starting to work?"

Tully glanced over at Alec. "That depends on the guy on my right. I asked him to come over tonight so we could put the screws to him."

"No pain so far," Alec said.

"Sarah says you're a heavy equipment operator, Alec, and that you worked county equipment once upon a time."

"That's right. But I'm an operator, not an owner."

"Want a job?"

"Not in any mine."

"You won't be off the seat of a 'dozer for sixty days. We'll pay going wages for a 'cat skinner' as long as we have an option on your services."

"That's for me," Alec said promptly. "Sure."

"This sounds a little nasty," Sam said, "but first you've got to get the bulldozer before you can seat him, Tully."

"I got it this afternoon," Tully said. "I called a contractor at Galena and rented one. I also rented a compressor here in town. The cat's on this afternoon's train and it'll be in to-night."

Sam Horne's eyebrows rose. "I thought you had to survey a road before you started to build it."

"I can run a hand level," Tully said. "All Alec will need are some grade stakes to go by, and a hand level is plenty accurate for that. Just so a four-wheel drive can get up and down it without too much grief."

Now Tully looked at Kevin. "Mr. Russel, are there six good miners in this town that the Mahaffey hasn't hired?"

"The best ones won't work for Hodes," Kevin said quietly. "There are more than six."

"Can we round them up by noon?" Tully asked. "I've got a cook already located—also a couple of wall tents and enough lumber for floors and sides. I got hold of a trailer this afternoon. We'll load it with a stove and the rest of this junk so when Alec pioneers the road with the 'dozer we can set up shop in a hurry. By the time Alec has made his second trip and picked up the compressor and hoist, we'll have a roof over the men and be ready to mine. By the time we've got the ore bin built, we should have something to put in it." He paused. "How does that sound?"

"Like you'd been operating," Sarah said. "Where was I when you were doing all this promoting?"

"You were taking down the immortal words of the county commissioners."

Sarah rose and moved to the stove where she looked into the coffeepot. Afterward, she began distributing old Kevin's cracked cups around the table.

"What have I forgotten, Mr. Russel, not counting powder, fuse and caps, and your own drilling and hoisting equipment?"

"We'd have use for a forge and coal," old Kevin said. "It would be a good idea if one of your miners is a blacksmith, too. You better get four hundred yards of inch pipe with enough sawdust to insulate it. You'll be that far from the creek if you make your camp at number one shaft."

Tully looked at Sam Horne and they grinned at each other. Then Tully said, "I'll do that." Afterward, Sarah poured the coffee and the talk went on. It was mostly mining talk and was concerned with the geology of the claims. His hand shaking, old Kevin drew for them on a piece of cheap tablet paper the course of the ore body as he had followed its exposures through the ten claims.

Tully listened attentively while Sam Horne, ignorant of everything but the most superficial mining talk, listened with open fascination. Presently, he drained his cup and shoved it toward the center of the table. "Rakes and drifts," he murmured, "foot walls and hanging walls, yakety-yak-yak-yak. Why does a miner have to use that double talk?" He rose then and reached for his coat, hanging over the back of his chair.

"When I was a boy," Kevin said softly, "you couldn't have worked on the *Nugget* without knowing it. Most of the news started out something like this, 'There was jubilation at the Dolly Gray today when Miners Pat Morrison and Kevin Russel, sinking from the Cork stope to a cross-cut on the ninth level, turned up a considerable body of ore that indicates sixty-three ounces of silver or better.' "

Sam Horne laughed then and said, "You've got me, old-timer. I'd better learn my trade if this is going to be a mining town again." Suddenly he frowned and moved around the table, and then his gaze settled on old Kevin. "Has this mine got a name yet, Mr. Russel?"

"Yes, sir," old Kevin said promptly. "It's the Sarah Moffit Mine."

Tully looked at Sarah, who was standing behind her chair. She was looking down at old Kevin, and then she moved over and put a hand on his shoulder. "I'd rather have your mine named after me than the Queen Elizabeth, pop," she said. "Thank you."

Sam Horne shrugged into his coat, muttering over and over, "The Sarah Moffit, the Sarah Moffit." Then he announced, "That's a prettier name than the Home Stake or the Camp Bird, Mr. Russel, even if it isn't in tradition."

"The largest nugget of silver ever mined—1840 pounds plus—came from a mine in Aspen, Colorado, called the Molly Gibson," old Kevin said slyly.

Sam Horne grinned. "Have I said anything right tonight?" he asked. "I'd better be going."

Tully knew he should be going, too, in order to give old Kevin his rest. He quickly settled the details of tomorrow's job with Alec and then rose, which was a signal for all of them to move into the living room.

Sarah gathered up the cups and rinsed them in the sink. Sam Horne, on his way out, called good night to her, and she answered him from the kitchen.

When she entered the living room Tully was holding her coat for her. As she slipped into it, Alec said, "The jeep's outside. Want a shaking up before you go to sleep?"

Sarah looked up at Tully. "I'd like to walk home if your flashlight will last that long, Tully."

"No takers, Alec. See you tomorrow," Tully said.

Alec went out, and afterwards Sarah and Tully said good night to Kevin, and stepped out into the cool evening. There was a bite of frost in the air, and they could hear the rush of the river, still sibilant with the runoff of yesterday's rain. It would probably be the last rain, Tully thought. Sarah slipped her arm through Tully's and, guided by the beam of their flashlight, they set out under the great cottonwoods on the weed-bordered path to town.

Tully was tired and he hoped that his legs would not choose the next few minutes to fail him again. He wondered idly if he should tell Sarah about this infirmity, and decided against it. Once it happened in her presence, it would be easy enough to explain to her, but the chances were it never would.

He was aware, now, that Sarah, beside him, was humming softly, and he glanced down at her in the dark. "You sound happy."

"I've got a mine named after me—a great big, rich mine."

"It'll bring us luck."

"Well, it always brought me luck." Sarah was silent a moment, as if thinking. "You know, it really has, even if I haven't stopped to think about it much."

Tully considered this a moment. Usually a fatherless young girl drudging at a dull job didn't consider herself especially lucky, and now Tully asked curiously, "How do you figure that?"

He felt Sarah's arm move against his as she shrugged. "Oh, I don't know. I had more fun when I was a kid than any ten girls I know. We lived in a big brick house like the Hodes house. I had bannisters to slide down, a big attic to hide in, two ponies, one black, one brown, and five Llewellyn setters to play with. My dad taught me how to fish dry flies and to hunt elk and how to run a trap line. Did you know I caught a lynx once?"

"Is that good?"

"Good? The pelt was in Harmer's window for over a year!"

"Then it must be good," Tully said, and they both laughed together.

There was an engaging simplicity about this girl that made Tully feel good, and for a moment his scheming, his worries and his dim sense of guilt were forgotten. He was trying to picture Sarah's childhood in this town, and there came to him a moment of envy. He asked curiously, "Was your dad in the mining business?"

"Mother's father was. Dad took over after he died. You probably never heard of the Hawley Mine. Dad ran it until the shaft got so deep he couldn't lick the water. We were in low-grade silver then and we couldn't buy new pumps. I remember the day he locked the office door. I was standing on the steps watching him. You know how you can feel sad sometimes without really knowing why you are. That was the way I felt then."

"Did he, too?"

Sarah didn't answer for a moment, then she said, "No. He took the keys out of the door and held them in his hand and just looked at them for a minute. Then he looked at me and his eyes weren't sad at all. You know what he did next?"

"No."

"He wound up like a baseball player and threw the keys as far as he could, then he said to me, 'Maybe now I can get that big cutthroat up above the Sawmill riffle. I never had time to really work on him before.'"

Tully smiled into the night. "He sounds like a good guy."

"He was. I told you I was lucky."

They were in town now and as Tully turned the corner toward the Moffit apartment, he saw the lights of the hotel a block ahead of them. He remembered then his first night here and the imperious girl in the red convertible. At the moment, he found it hard to connect her with Sarah Moffit.

They turned on the stairs of the Moffit apartment and slowly climbed them arm in arm. There was only a dim light at the far end of the corridor, Tully saw, when they achieved the top of the stairs and halted before the door to Sarah's apartment.

Sarah put out her hand and Tully took it.

"I'd ask you in, but I'm a working girl." She smiled and added, "As of tomorrow you're a working lad, too."

"The proletariat has to stand together," Tully said mockingly. And on impulse he took her in his arms and kissed her. There was no resistance, but little cooperation from Sarah. Tully heard the apartment door open and the hall was suddenly flooded with light. A kind of anger at being thus surprised stirred in Tully; he let the kiss linger a moment longer and then broke slowly away from Sarah, expecting to be confronted by a surprised Mrs. Moffit.

Instead, his glance rested on Ben Hodes hulking in the open doorway. Sarah turned slowly, deliberately, as if also resenting this invasion of her privacy. Tully said dryly, "Are you the new truant officer?"

"Don't let me disturb you," Hodes said, his voice sardonic and angry.

"You are. Shut the door."

"That's enough," Sarah said matter-of-factly. "What're you doing here, Ben?"

"Watching you kiss Gibbs." Hodes's voice held a sullen resentment. "I came over to see you, and your mother told me you were out. I decided to wait, so she went to bed. When I heard your footsteps on the stairs and then no sound at all, I opened the door." He added in a sour attempt at humor, "You were both being naughty."

Sarah shouldered past him and walked swiftly into the living room. For a moment Tully stood undecided on the threshold and then he thought, *I'll be damned if I leave her this way,* and stepped into the room. Hodes moved to block his entrance and Sarah said sharply, "Come in, both of you."

Hodes stepped aside reluctantly. Tully walked over to Sarah. He heard Ben close the door and follow him into the room. Without turning, he said to Sarah, "I know you're tired. You want me to throw this snoop out of here?"

Sarah did not look at Ben; she regarded Tully with something like affection, and there was a sudden mischief in her eyes. "No, I'll take care of him, Tully. Good night." And then, surprisingly, she came up to him and kissed him squarely on the lips.

For an amazed second Tully stood there and then Sarah spoke over his shoulder. "I'll kiss whoever I want, Ben, whether you're spying on me or not."

"So I notice," Hodes said sullenly. "Maybe a man has to have a Silver Star, a couple of broken legs and fainting spells before you'll kiss him."

"Do you have fainting spells, Tully?" Sarah asked.

"You mean he hasn't told you?" Ben asked.

"Told me what?" Sarah looked at Tully in puzzlement.

"Let him tell it," Tully said.

"Sometimes his legs don't work," Ben said sourly. "That's one way of making a bid for sympathy. I'm surprised he hasn't pulled it on you, Sarah."

"They're working now," Tully said flatly. "Want me to prove it?"

"I don't want you to prove anything," Sarah said hastily.

Tully said to Ben now, "Why don't you shut up? Even better, why don't you leave? You want it spelled out for you?"

Hodes took a step toward them and halted. "Look—" he began heavily when Sarah cut in with an unaccustomed curtness. "Yes, why don't you?"

Baffled, Hodes looked from one to the other. "I was invited in here by your mother."

Sarah said tartly, "All right, wake her up and visit with her."

"But what have I done?"

Tully said quietly, "You've eavesdropped, my friend. The next time you do it I'll drop an eave on you." He glanced obliquely at Sarah. "We're going now, Sarah—Hodes and I." To Hodes he said, "Lead off, friend. You know where the door is."

For an angry moment Hodes regarded him, then shifted his attention to Sarah. "I think you kissed him to spite me."

"That's perceptive of you, Ben. You'd better leave or I'll kiss him again." Wordlessly Hodes turned, walked over to a chair, picked up his hat, then turned to look sadly at Sarah.

"Don't trip on your lip," Tully prodded.

Hodes only said sorrowfully, "Good night, Sarah," and headed for the door.

Tully glanced at Sarah, "I've already said good night, I guess." He grinned, turned and followed Hodes out. Closing the door behind him, he observed that Hodes was waiting on the top step. Tully walked toward him and the two of them silently descended the stairs.

Once on the sidewalk below, Hodes halted and put out a hand as if to restrain Tully, who stopped short of him, a wariness upon him.

"Don't ever do that again," Hodes said slowly.

"I'll do it every chance I get."

"She's my girl," Hodes said flatly.

"So you said. But that's not the way the votes count out."

"Just take this as a warning," Hodes said deliberately. "You've come in here a cute little war hero, you've parlayed one of my mistakes into a partnership in a mine, but Sarah doesn't go with the property. Don't make the mistake of thinking she does."

With that he turned and walked off into the night.

After leaving Tully, Hodes stopped in at the Elks Club. It was a Monday night and the club rooms were almost deserted. He tramped through the reading room, and went into the empty barroom. Here he poured a drink from his own bottle, checked the billiard room and found it empty, then took his drink in, turned on the lights, pulled off his coat and set about playing a solo game of billiards.

It just didn't take. In his memory, he kept seeing Sarah in Tully's arms, and when he finally, with a violence that he could not control, drove two balls off the table, he racked his cue and sat down heavily in an armchair against the wall. Someone in the distant reading room coughed, but Ben sat silent, sipping at his drink, an angry bafflement within him.

In the past two days the whole pattern of his life had changed for him. It seemed to him that all he had liked and grown used to and accepted as his own was now threatened —and by a complete stranger. The Vicksburg Claims were slipping away from him, and more important, so was Sarah. It had taken him two years of solid dating, countless dinners, and a hundred grudging apologies to get his first kiss from Sarah. At that it had been a sisterly, half-mocking kiss. It had taken Gibbs just three days.

Ben looked at his glass and found it empty. He tramped back into the bar, mixed himself a fresh and stronger one, and then, for fear he would be intruded upon, he retreated again to his chair in the billiard room. Slacking into the chair he relaxed, tilted his head back and closed his eyes, feeling the glass pleasantly cold in his fist. He decided now that he would have to act decisively or everything would be lost. This afternoon, to check Byers's story of what went on in the commissioner's meeting, he had told Olive Lindsay to call the Uinta Construction Company in Galena to check if a bulldozer had been ordered by Gibbs. It had not only been ordered, but it had been loaded on that day's train and was probably on the Azurite siding right now.

Carefully, now, Ben considered what advantages lay with him and the Mahaffey. Tully had a hundred and twenty days to build a road and move enough high-grade ore to the mill and smelter to pay back the ten-thousand-dollar loan. If he didn't—

Ben sat up, opening his eyes, the idea dawning on him. If Tully couldn't repay the loan, then Ben could attach his assets. And his assets were a share in the Vicksburg Claims. *That's it,* Ben thought delightedly. His obvious move was to put every possible obstruction in the way of Tully's completing the road and moving the ore. Ben spent five more seconds considering the man to do the job, and when he had him, he moved.

He glanced briefly at his watch, put on his coat, snapped out the billiard-room light and left the club. Out in the night he turned left at the first cross street, heading for the least prosperous section of town against the mountains. Here the town seemed darker and the street lamps farther apart—or maybe it was because this was the working-class section of town and working stiffs went to bed early. A dog picked him up, barking furiously, and Ben managed to kick him. Once the yelps of the retreating dog fell off, it was utterly quiet, and his footfalls on the gravel road sounded loud enough to wake the dead.

At a dark intersection, made more confusing by the absence of a street light and by the emergence of two crooked alleys, Ben halted to take his bearings. Then he moved angling into the narrowest alley and tramped down it between rotting sheds until he came to a small, dark building abutting the alley whose painted window frames loomed gray in the black night. The building was unlighted. For a moment Ben hesitated, then he moved toward it, stumbling over a heap of cans before he reached the door.

He knocked loudly and waited. Presently, a sleep-dulled voice called through the door, "Get the hell away from here!"

"It's me, Ben Hodes. Let me in, Arnie." There was a sound of movement in the shack, then a light went on and the door opened. A gangling figure in rumpled underdrawers and shirt stood in the doorway. This was Arnie Lind.

"Come in, Ben, come in. I thought you was a drunk on his way home."

Ben stepped into the squalid kitchen-bedroom which smelled of bacon grease and unclean bedding. Arnie shut the door behind him, then moved barefoot over to the chair over which his pants were draped.

He removed the pants, swung the chair out, and said, "Sit down, Ben."

Ben eased himself into the chair, regarding Arnie, who was a wiry but big-boned Finn with a thatch of thick iron-gray hair topping a wedge-shaped face. His hands were huge and permanently grease-stained, since he was a machinist at the Mahaffey mill. Ben had chosen him for a number of reasons, among which was the fact that he lived and drank alone and that Ben's father, years ago, had got him out of a serious knifing scrape. Arnie was, Ben knew, reliable up to a point, thoroughly dishonest and sufficiently taciturn.

When Arnie, still barefoot but wearing pants now, sat down on the edge of the bed, Ben saw that his small, pale eyes, cunning as a homeless dog's, were regarding him with covert speculation.

"Something break down at the mill?" Arnie inquired.

Ben shook his head impatiently. He wished he had some other seat than this frail chair so nakedly in the open. Rising, he moved the chair almost against the wall, unbuttoned his coat, sat down, tilted his chair back and offered Arnie a cigarette. Arnie accepted it, lit Ben's cigarette and then his own and settled back on the bed again, watching Ben.

"Arnie," Ben began, "I've got a new job for you."

A faint alarm seemed to come in Arnie's face. "You mean you don't like my work?"

"This has nothing to do with the mill," Ben said. "I want a man I can trust, a man who won't talk, and a man with some sense, and I'll pay well."

"For what?" Arnie asked.

Ben considered his cigarette a moment, wondering whether to give Arnie the whole story. He decided he'd have to if Arnie was to operate with any understanding of what was required of him. Accordingly, he told Arnie of Tully Gibbs's new partnership with Kevin Russel to mine the Vicksburg Claims. He related with complete candor his own ambitions to get those claims for the Mahaffey.

This was something Arnie could appreciate, and he grinned faintly as Ben went on to tell of Gibbs's appeal for county help, of the commissioners' refusal and of Gibbs's renting equipment from the Galena firm.

"You see how it is," Ben explained. "This Gibbs is racing against winter. He's got a hell of a job getting in that road, and he hasn't got the really big dough to rent lots of equipment and swing it in a hurry." He paused, "I want you to see that he doesn't get it in."

Arnie, not committing himself, was silent.

"There's a hundred things you can do, Arnie," Ben went on. "You can find out what equipment he's rounding up here and foul it up. When we find out who's working for him, maybe we can reach them. Understand, I don't want anybody hurt, but I want him to run into so much grief that he'll be absolutely stalled. How does it sound?"

Arnie inhaled deeply on his cigarette, staring at the floor, and then he shrugged. "I got a job to take care of, Ben."

"I thought of that," Ben said. "Tomorrow send Everett around to check that motor on three level. Armstrong has been beefing about it for days. When he's out of the shop, pretend you dropped something on your hand. Get it bandaged up, come in to me and ask to go see Doc Richards. That'll give you three or four days off. Hang around town and see what you can find out about Gibbs's plans. Check with me and then do the job at night. How about it?"

Ben saw the sly amusement mount into Arnie's eyes. Once the economic side of it was taken care of, Ben guessed, the natural inclination to delinquency in Arnie would conquer.

"Okay with me," Arnie said softly. "When do I start?"

"Before you take it, Arnie, I want one thing understood. You're off work with a hurt hand. If you damn well don't stay out of the saloons, I'll can you from the mill."

Arnie grinned in understanding. "Okay. When do I start?"

"Tonight."

By the time Beth Hodes had the dinner dishes washed up and the kitchen spotless, Ben had left the house. She had no idea where he'd gone and cared even less. Snapping out the kitchen light, she walked through the dining room, straightened one of the heavy Victorian chairs as she circled the table, and entered the living room. There was the whole evening—*a manless evening*, she thought—before her. She lifted a cigarette from the coffee table and put it between her lips, but did not light it. It came to her with the weight of weary depression that this very act, in this very room, at this very hour had been repeated a thousand times, and would be repeated another thousand.

She wondered bitterly what would happen if she went to the phone, called up Frank Nichols, Sam Horne, or even Tully Gibbs and asked them to drop over for a drink. With a kind of wry self-derision she thought, *Nobody in his right mind invites a beating from Ben.*

Listlessly then, she lighted her cigarette, wondering how to occupy herself the rest of the evening. All the household chores were done for the day; she'd read all this week's magazines and she had seen the movie last night. She could wash her hair, but the thought bored her. Idly she walked over to the phone and called the Moffit apartment, thinking a round of Canasta might appeal to Sarah. Mrs. Moffit, however, informed her that Sarah was out, and Beth boredly cradled the phone.

But a deep restlessness was upon her. She turned down the living-room lights, got a coat from the hall closet and stepped out into the pleasant night. At the end of the walk she paused undecided, and then turned left toward the outskirts of town. She admitted to herself that this was a measure of her desperation; it was a spinster's substitute for working off energy that should be channeled into working with a man, raising his children and looking after a family. She walked briskly now, taking consistent left turns, so that in an hour she had half circled the town and found herself at the far south end of Main Street.

Tired now, she turned up Main and into the dim-lit business section. So far this evening she had met no one, and it only deepened her fancy, which sometimes almost amounted to a fear, that she was living a life hermetically sealed from the realities of other people. As she passed the hotel she heard the lobby door open behind her and a man's voice said, "Why, hello, Beth!"

Beth halted, turned and saw that it was Sam Horne who had spoken. She smiled pleasantly and said, "Evening, Sam!" It had been so long since she had used her voice that it sounded rusty and harsh, and she felt a small enbarrassment.

"If I didn't know who it was, I'd swear you were a dame looking for a pickup," Sam said. He came over to her and she saw his faint, wry smile.

Remembering yesterday, Beth found it hard to meet his glance, but she decided to adopt his own flip tone of voice. "How do you know I'm not?"

Sam slipped his arm through hers and said, "All right. You've made the grade," and fell in beside her. His easy manner thawed Beth. She glanced curiously at him, and saw nothing but friendliness in his face. It was as if he had already forgotten yesterday's unpleasantness. "I'm a working man and I can't stand much carousing," Sam said. "Will you settle for a cup of coffee and a doughnut?"

"Two doughnuts. I think I've walked three miles tonight."

Sam glanced briefly at her. "That business yesterday upset you?"

"Shouldn't it have?"

Sam didn't answer. He steered her into the empty restaurant and gestured toward a booth at the right wall. When they were seated, he ordered from the aproned cook, and then settled back against the booth. Beth, knowing he was watching her, busied herself by taking a cigarette from her purse and lighting it.

"You know, I hate coffee," Sam said irrelevantly. "But I keep drinking it. Kevin Russel already fed me five cups tonight, and here I am again." He pulled an earlobe, scowling. "I wish I liked something else to drink besides alcohol."

Beth laughed in spite of herself.

Sam said abruptly, "You know, you're damned pretty, Beth. Anyone ever tell you that?"

Beth started, and then thought, *I'm damned if I'll blush.* "My mother did once."

Sam snorted. "No man has?"

Beth smiled faintly and shook her head in negation.

"That's right. Ben never gives you a chance to hear one, does he?"

A sudden discomfort came to Beth, and she could not hold Sam's friendly gaze.

"Well, a man just has. You can tell that to Ben."

"I don't think I will," Beth said softly.

"You mean you think he'd beat me up?"

"Something like that."

The cook interrupted them with their coffee and doughnuts. Sam ladled three spoonsfuls of sugar into his coffee, grimaced at the glazed doughnuts and pushed them away from him, then folded his arms on the table top and said conversationally, "You know, you're one of the few women I know who's scared. You read these crummy three-name-female authoresses in the rental library and they've always got their heroines cowering in the corner because some nasty man is threatening them. They're so damn delicate and sensitive." He scowled thoughtfully and said, "Actually that's strictly laughing gas. Women are tougher than hell, and they don't scare easy. They're not like you. You'd make a damn good cornball heroine."

As Beth listened, her anger began to rise. She knew Sam saw it, because he smiled. "Your next line should be 'I didn't come here to be insulted,' just in case you're reaching for it."

"I'm not reaching for a line. I'm just listening," Beth said coldly.

"Thereby admitting it's true?"

"I guess."

"Then why the hell don't you do something about it?" Sam asked.

Beth felt a real anger pushing her. "What do you suggest I do, shoot him?"

"That's an unclean thought. Purge yourself of it," Sam said soberly. His tone of voice was just as sober, but it held more vehemence as he said, "Get out of that big house, Beth! Get a room! Get a job! Cook your own meals and ask the boys up to the place. If Ben bothers you, call in the law. You're over twenty-one and fancy free, at least in theory."

The truth of his words galled Beth deeply. In effect, what Sam was saying was that instead of wallowing in self-pity, she should do something about her present life. And so she should. She was aware now of the gentleness in Sam's eyes behind his glasses, and she knew there had been no malice in his words.

"You're just lazy," Sam said accusingly. "You're—"

Beth cut in. "I can finish it, Sam. I'm used to good living, and I like our house."

Sam nodded. "You like it well enough to put up with what happened yesterday?"

"I'm sorry about that."

"No, you're not." Sam's voice was rough. "If you were, you'd do something about it."

"But what can I do? All I know how to do is cook and

keep house. The only reason I learned that is because I was bored."

"Got any money?"

"Enough to keep me. So what do I do—rent a dirty little room and buy a gas plate?"

"You get a job. After that the room won't seem dirty and you won't mind the gas plate."

Sam reached up and removed his glasses, then flipped a paper napkin open and proceeded to clean them with it. He scowled at the coffee cup while he vigorously cleaned them. Suddenly he said, "Can you spell?"

"Yes."

Sam seemed startled. "That's the first positive statement I ever heard you make."

"All right. But I can."

"Then how'd you like to work for me?"

Beth looked at him searchingly. A wild hope stirred within her for a moment and then it died. This, she understood instinctively, was a gesture stemming from pity. Her glance fell away from Sam, and she said, "Thanks, Sam, but I can't write, and you know it."

Sam laughed, and put his glasses back on. "You're not supposed to. All you'll do for a long time is write items like this: 'Oscar Johnson, the Misses Tillie and Georgia Johnson were visitors to Galena last Saturday.' Just so you spell their names right."

Beth only smiled, and Sam went on, "I'll pay you thirty bucks a week, more than I can afford."

Beth knew that Sam was exaggerating the simplicity of the job. She also knew that he was doing this in part out of pity for her and in part out of liking for her. If she could pay her way, the pity would vanish, and the liking would remain. Lest he reconsider, she said recklessly, "I'll take it."

"On one condition. You move out of that house first."

"I'll do that, too."

Sam reached for the check and stood up. "Come on, I'll take you home. I'll probably try to kiss you, too, so start worrying about that."

* * *

Alec was dressed in a clean pair of green army mechanic's coveralls, and, perhaps with the prospect of a steady paycheck in sight, his pocket bulged with a handful of cigars, one of which he expertly fired up as he drove.

Tully marshaled in his mind the chores ahead of him today. They would unload the cat in plenty of time to avoid a demurrage charge and then assemble their equipment by trailer. In the meantime he must round up a crew, one of whom would come with him in Alec's jeep tomorrow to serve as level rodman for putting in the grade stakes. It was Tully's guess that by the following day Alec would have all the gear assembled and would start pioneering the new road.

Approaching the spur now, Alec saw the big yellow fifteen-ton bulldozer resting on the flatcar. When they swung into the cinder-strewn siding, Alec braked to a stop and regarded the towering cat. "Nearly new," Alec said approvingly.

Tully, however, was already looking ahead of them. He spied the pile of ties mentioned by the station agent in their conversation yesterday. To unload the cat they must first shore up the near side of the flatcar and build a ramp to the ground. For this, Tully had asked permission to use the ties.

"Let's break our backs first," Tully said, and reluctantly put the jeep in motion toward the pile of ties.

They worked most of the morning hauling ties to the flatcar and bracing it against the moment when the monstrous weight of the cat would begin to tip it. That completed, they used more ties to construct a wide sloping ramp to the ground. Sometime after midday they took twenty minutes to drive back to town for food, and then returned to the siding. By this time they were both grimy with creosote from the ties. After a final survey, they swung onto the flatcar to warm up the cat's motor. Alec stepped up onto the seat and then out onto the tread. Tully, checking the winch cable, suddenly heard Alec's startled profanity and he glanced up.

Alec was looking at him. "Come get a load of this!"

Tully climbed over the seat and joined Alec on the tread,

and he saw Alec pointing mutely at the fuel pump. Its top was cracked and smashed, its sides stained by leaking diesel oil. Tully swore softly under his breath and knelt to examine it. There was no mistaking the damage. It looked as if someone had taken a sledge to the pump.

Alec reached out and lifted a shattered bit of metal from the caved-in housing. Then he glanced at Tully, both wrath and bitterness in his dark eyes. "What you figure?"

Tully said grimly, "Looks like somebody took a sledge to it." He looked at Alec. "What's the roadbed like between here and Galena? Could a rock have fallen on it in one of those canyons?"

"Rock, hell!" Alec said angrily. "Funny it would pick the fuel pump to fall on." His glance held Tully's. "Who knew it was coming?"

Tully rose and, hands on hips, frowned in thought. "That's just it, nobody."

"Where'd you call from?"

"The pay phone in the hotel lobby. Nobody was there, not even the clerk. I had to go next door to get change."

Alec shook his head. "Somebody knew it would be here." Now he rose, too.

"What'll it do to us?" Tully asked.

"Gimme a minute," Alec said sourly. He swung off the flatcar, ducked under it and lugged his toolbox out of the jeep. Tully helped him swing it onto the car, and then Alec went to work dismounting the fuel pump, Tully gloomily watching and helping when he could.

In a little while they knew the extent of the damage. It was not a thorough job of wrecking, as if whoever did the furtive job was in a hurry. When at last Alec assessed the damage, Tully said flatly, "All right, let's get on the phone. They may have repairs in Galena."

The ride back to town was a silent one. Tully directed Alec to drive to the courthouse, and then lapsed into gloomy silence. The whole thing made no sense to him. Only Alec, Sam Horne, Sarah and Kevin knew about the cat coming. It was true the station agent could have known and informed Hodes. Tully would check with Sarah on the agent.

Sarah was at a ledger when Alec and Tully stalked in. She looked from one grim face to the other as they halted at the counter, and said, "Something's wrong, I can tell."

Briefly Tully described the condition in which they had found the cat. Then he asked, "What about the station agent, Sarah? Would he tattle to Hodes once he saw the bill of lading?"

"Ollie Harnes?" Sarah asked in surprise. "Hardly. Ben has made his life so miserable in shipping concentrates that he hates him."

Alec nodded. "That's out."

"Then how did Hodes know?" Tully demanded.

The three of them looked at each other in silence. "Well," Sarah said slowly, "an RD-7 isn't easy to hide."

"The train got in after midnight," Alec said. "I was awake when it whistled."

"You don't walk up to a cat with a sledge in your hand and wreck it in broad daylight," Tully said. "It must have been at night. Who knew it would be in?"

There was no answer to that, and now Tully wearily skirted the counter. "Sarah, can I make a call from your phone and pay the charges?"

Sarah nodded, and Tully pulled a blank piece of paper in front of him, picked up a pencil and began to list the parts needed. When he had questioned Alec for additional needs, he picked up the phone and called the construction company at Galena.

It took less than a minute to get a connection and Tully first checked on the condition of the cat when it left yesterday. Since it was loaded under its own power, they informed him, the fuel pump could hardly be defective. Then Tully read from his list and asked if the parts were in stock. When they asked him for further details, he handed the phone to Alec, who rattled off the desired information. Standing above him, Tully listened. Finally Alec looked up at Tully and only grinned and nodded.

Finally Alec said into the phone, "I'll take off in an hour. I'll get there sometime tonight. Where can I pick the stuff up?"

Details settled, Alec hung up and said, "We couldn't have been luckier. They've had fuel pump trouble on one of their RD-7's, so they'd ordered a whole new unit that hasn't been installed. It's in their stockroom." He rose, lifted a cigar from the breast pocket of his coveralls and lighted it. "I can borrow a car and start right now. I'll be back in the middle of the morning."

Tully said, "Hold on a minute." He picked up the phone, checked the long-distance charges, counted money out on the desk and then looked briefly at Sarah. "See you later."

When Tully and Alec had gone, Sarah walked slowly over to the desk and sat down. There was no doubt in her mind that Ben Hodes was behind this sabotage of the cat, but how he had learned of its coming baffled her. She stared, musing, at the change Tully had left on the desk, and then reached out to pick it up.

As she did so her glance fell on the list of repairs Tully had written. Her hand halted, and then gently settled to the desk top as she studied the handwriting. *Where've I seen this writing before?* she wondered. It was a curious, delicate, slanting engineer's calligraphy with its own peculiar way of inserting oddly formed capital letters in unexpected places. It was as individual as a thumbprint.

For still seconds she searched her memory, and then it came to her with shattering abruptness. This was the handwriting of the letters which Kevin Russel had received from his son, Jimmy, when he was in the hospital.

For an aching minute Sarah considered the implications of this knowledge. Tully had written those letters for Jimmy —letters in which Lieutenant Tully Gibbs had been praised as a friend and a hero. In one bleak moment Sarah, remembering that Tully had denied any knowledge of the letters, knew that he had composed them and used them to obtain a half interest in the Vicksburg Claims and the Sarah Moffit Mine.

5

Sarah wakened reluctantly to her mother's gentle scolding coming from above her.

"All right, Ma," she said in a voice slurred with sleep.

"You're sure you'll get up this time?"

"Uh-huh." She heard her mother's footsteps retreat and she lay a moment looking at the ceiling, her pale hair spread awry on the pillow, feeling the depression settle on her spirits once more. She had finally fallen asleep just before dawn, after endless hours of tormented indecision. First she had wondered if she could confront Tully with her evidence of his crookedness. She further wondered if she should tell Kevin. The answer to that, of course, was no. Knowledge that Tully had defrauded him would probably kill the old man. Was it better, she wondered, to keep silent and pile up evidence of Tully's further dishonesty or should she speak up and halt this swindle now? Beyond that, she had begun to like a man who was an unprincipled crook.

She flung the covers aside, irritable with the knowledge that she was as bewildered and uncertain this morning as she had been last night. It was in the middle of her shower that the answer came to her. Why not lay the whole thing before Sam Horne? It was really evading the issue, but Sam might be able to help.

Her mother had laid out her breakfast before she left for work. Sarah turned on the radio in the sunny kitchen and as she ate she listened to the hearty voice of the announcer spread the daily portion of gloom.

She did not let the fact she was late for work hurry her. Now she had arrived at some sort of decision she felt relieved and lazy and hungry. She was also melancholy.

It was almost the middle of a sunny, crisp morning when she stepped onto the street. She noted immediately that the first of the red-garbed hunters were arriving in town for hunting season. Azurite was in the heart of the elk country, but what had once been a local sport had lately assumed the proportions of a plague. Sarah knew that within the next couple or three days, scores of trucks with trailers hauling horses, baled hay and even jeeps would swarm into town. The firing range up beyond the city dump would be booming from dawn to dusk as hunters sighted in their guns. On opening day the town again would be deserted, the hunters having taken to the hills. Shortly afterwards the reverse process would occur; the trucks and jeeps, loaded with game lashed to fenders or lying stiffly in truck beds, would pass through town headed for home. Before the season ended chances were that at least one hunter would be killed or that a search party would have to be mustered from the weary but helpful townspeople to find a lost hunter. Time was, Sarah thought, when hunting was the most carefree time of the year, when hunting was the province of hunters. Now, anyone who had the price of a gun was a hunter; skill and woodcraft counted for nothing. The woods were full of hunters who shot at anything that moved or made a sound and in turn, risked death or mutilation from their fellow hunters. I *am* depressed, she thought.

Two blocks down the street she stepped into the dark, ink-smelling, single long room that housed the *Azurite Nugget.* The first thing she saw was Beth Hodes seated at a new rolltop desk jammed up against the far wall behind the counter. When the door swung shut behind Sarah, Beth looked around.

"Hi, Beth," Sarah said. "What's this, the new waiting room?"

"No such thing," Beth answered, and smiled shyly. "This is my working desk."

Sarah's lips parted a little in amazement. "You're working here?"

Beth nodded.

"Good girl!" Sarah exclaimed, then added, "What did you do, poison Ben?"

"I didn't have to. I moved out." The two girls looked at each other with understanding.

"Did he hit you?" Sarah asked then. Beth rose and came over to the counter and Sarah noticed that there was a lingering excitement in Beth's eyes.

"I moved all my clothes over to Mrs. Kelly's yesterday afternoon. I left a note for Ben telling him I'd taken a room there." She started to giggle now, and then continued, "He came rampaging over after work. Mrs. Kelly met him with a poker, ordered him off the place and locked the door. I haven't seen him this morning, but I expect he'll be around."

Sarah was laughing, too, now. Then her face sobered and she said earnestly. "Make it stick, Beth. You've got to make it stick. If you don't now, you never will again."

"I know that," Beth murmured. "Whenever I feel myself weakening, I remember Frank Nichols. I remember—" She broke off, and shrugged. "If I don't make it stick, I'll buy a ring for my nose. But I will!"

Sarah patted her hand lightly and it was at once a gesture of belief and sympathy and reassurance. "I believe you."

She looked down the room now and saw Sam in conference with the linotype operator. He was in shirt sleeves and a soiled denim apron was tied around his ample middle. When Sarah halted beside him he looked up from a sheet of yellow copy paper that he and Ed Small, the bespectacled linotype operator, had been studying. "Hi, Sarah," Sam said gloomily. Then he nodded toward the front. "When I hired her, she said she could spell. Look at this. Chlorophyl with one l."

"It has one l," Sarah said.

"It has two," Sam said belligerently. Then he added with less truculence, "You sure about that?"

"It's optional, I think," Sarah said.

"You think!"

"Don't bully me, Sam Horne," Sarah said warningly. "I'm not working for you. As a matter of fact, if you jump on Beth the first day she'll probably go back to Ben Hodes."

Ed Small laughed. "You tell him, Sarah. This is the only newspaper office in the country that hasn't got a dictionary. We just take a vote on words we don't know."

"I can spell," Sam said aggressively.

"We just had a demonstration," Sarah said dryly. "Come on, Sam. Let's go out back and have a smoke."

Sam, smiling at his own discomfiture, led the way past the composing table, the type cases and the job press out into the furnace room at the rear.

The walls of this room were papered with a hundred yellowing job press samples of posters, hand bills and auction notices printed on paper of all colors. It gave an oddly gay air to the room which held besides the big metal furnace a cluster of all the things that Sam could not bear to throw away. Strewn about was wrecked furniture, broken tools, gummy paint cans, half-empty bottles and, in a far corner, a mound of inextricably tangled wire coat hangers. A black, leather-covered overstuffed rocking chair rose as an island out of the litter. An old copy of the Sunday New York *Herald Tribune* kept its seat springs from impaling its occupant, and now Sam steered Sarah toward it. Beside it stood a rickety table. Sam, putting a leg up on it, offered Sarah a cigarette which she declined. Sam lighted his own and then said, "What's the new grief?"

"How do you know there is any?"

"You're too phony cheerful for this hour. Besides, you should be at work. Besides, I could get a couple of bowling balls in the bags under your eyes."

Sarah sighed. "All right, Sam, it's grief." She stretched out her long legs and crossed them, and then began her story. She told Sam of Tully's courthouse call to Galena for the bulldozer parts, saying that before he made the call he had made a list of the needed repairs. She went on to tell Sam of how Tully had left payment for the call on the desk and that in picking it up she had glanced at the list he'd written. The handwriting, she said, was the handwriting of the letters Kevin Russel had received from Jimmy while he was in the hospital.

When she finished, she only looked at Sam. He was staring searchingly at her, his cigarette burning unheeded in the corner of his mouth, a hard intelligence in his eyes.

Slowly then he reached up for the cigarette and murmured wryly, "That's a cutie—a real cutie."

"Isn't it? Do you see what he's done, Sam?"

Sam nodded. "He's cut himself a piece of cake." He smiled again.

"How could he do it, Sam? How could he?" Sarah asked vehemently.

"These kids nowdays get awfully hungry for money," Sam said. "I just didn't think he was that kind."

"But to prey on poor old Kevin!"

Sam looked at her sharply. "Wait a minute. Tully put up the only loot that's been put up, didn't he?"

"In return he got a half interest in a mine, didn't he?"

Sam didn't answer immediately, then he said slowly, haltingly, "Yeah, but there are degrees of dishonesty. If he pulls this off, he'll make Kevin halfway rich. That was your idea, wasn't it?"

"But look how he's going about it!" Sarah countered. "It's detestable. Praising himself, bragging about himself, lying his way into Kevin's confidence—lying until I wonder his teeth don't turn black!"

"Well, I wouldn't recommend his type for a scout master," Sam conceded. "Still, you can't hang him for it."

Sarah leaned forward now. "How can we believe anything about him now, Sam? Do we really know he's a mining engineer? How do we know he didn't steal this money he put up? How do we know he'll even give Kevin his rightful share?"

"Whoa," Sam cut in. "This is a partnership. Old Judge Hardy has drawn up the papers."

"You mean it's too late?"

Sam was already shaking his head in negation. "For Kevin to back out? Why should he?" He rose, dropped his cigarette on the floor, stepped on it, then ran his hands deep in his apron pockets. He walked slowly over to the furnace, stared at it thoughtfully, then kicked it. Wheeling, he came back to Sarah, a ferocious scowl on his face.

"Look, kid," he began, "we've got to be smart about this, because it might hurt a lot of people. Let's look at the facts. Kevin, for the first time, is going to have a good operating mine. He's put up nothing but the ore underground in that mine and some equipment. Tully, on the other hand, has put up ten thousand bucks. Add to that he seems to know what he's doing. In a partnership, books are audited and money is accounted for. A double signature on a check and endorsements will stop any fancy stuff." He spread his hands, palms upward, and shrugged. "Why wake it up?"

"Because Tully's dishonest!" Sarah said hotly. "If he's dishonest in one thing, he'll be the same in another!"

"Between us, we'll keep a tight check on him."

Sarah rose now. She shook her head vehemently. "But that's not right, Sam! He's a crook." She halted as if something important had occurred to her. "Why, how do we know he was a Marine flyer? How do we know he was even decorated? Couldn't he have heard about Kevin's mine and simply mailed those letters from San Diego claiming to be Jimmy's pilot?"

Sam thought a minute. "That's possible, except you forget one thing. The Marine guard at Jimmy's funeral mentioned his name and said he'd been awarded the Navy Cross."

"Ha!" Sarah said scornfully. "I'll believe anything now. I'll believe even a Marine guard can be bought. After all, wasn't that brat of a Jimmy a Marine?"

Sam leaned against the table again and regarded her thoughtfully. "You're a little mite suspicious this morning, aren't you?"

"Wouldn't you be?"

Sam nodded, but said nothing.

"Then what do we do, Sam?" Sarah's voice was insistent.

"Just watch—and keep it away from Kevin."

"That's not good enough for me," Sarah said soberly. "I'm going to find out about this Gibbs character, one way or another."

Sam was silent a long moment, then said slowly, "I'm going to do a little gumshoeing myself. The thing that interests me most is where he got the ten G's to invest in Kevin's claims."

"How will you do it?"

Sam shrugged. "How will you find out about him?"

"I don't know either, but I'll find a way."

Sam said slyly, "They say love always does."

The color mounted into Sarah's face and she glared angrily at Sam, not knowing that her feelings had been so close to the surface that Sam had read them. At last she said, "All right, Sam, that's another thing, too."

Sam rose and Sarah turned back toward the shop. She had reached the composing room door when Sam said with an odd gentleness, "Don't go off half cocked. Once you do, the pie has hit the fan."

Sarah halted and turned to look at him. "That's a strange thing to say."

Sam only shook his head. "Well, it's a strange situation, isn't it?"

For a moment Sarah was tempted to give a bitter retort in answer, and then she checked herself and went on toward the door.

The camp Tully had set up on the Vicksburg Claims was at shaft Number One. In two days Alec had pioneered the road with the bulldozer as far as the last pitch with a trailerful of lumber, pipe, grub, bedding and tools.

Leaving the grade stakes at the last pitch, they had bushwhacked their way around to the back of the ridge to Number One shaft and unloaded the trailer. Already the floored cookshack and wall tent were up, and a chainsaw crew was clearing timber for the road and cutting timbers for the ore bin.

In midafternoon Tully, who was laying pipe through the timber from the creek to the camp, lifted his head to listen. Dimly he heard the deep-throated thrashing of the distant cat, and he said to Bill Ligon, his helper, "Here's Alec with the compressor." Tully rose and moved over to pick up a length of pipe which the cat had spotted as its first chore.

He was shirtless and the sun felt suddenly warm on his back as he tramped through a patch of sunlight. These three days since Alec had returned with repairs had been driving daylight-to-dark sessions, with little time out for rest or food. His road survey had been easy and swift and Alec had experienced no great difficulties on the pioneer trip. Except for water, the camp was habitable and Tully meant to spend little time in improving it. With the coming of the compressor he could put his miners to work tomorrow, leaving the rest of the crew to finish the ore bin and to cut the cribbing logs for the road.

By the time he had tightened the joint of the next pipe, the sound of the cat had become a sustained chatter out on the timber to the east. Rising, Tully listened to the beat of the motor. The compressor was a heavy load for the twisting bushwhack trail that Alec was forced to use until the road could be completed. He heard the sudden gunning of the motor and the deeper roar of the 'dozer, and knew that Alec was on the last grade approaching camp. Picking up his shirt, he said to Bill, "Let's knock off with this, and unload the compressor."

They tramped back through the big and scattered spruces toward camp, arriving just as Alec cut the motor. The camp itself lay at the edge of the timber, the two tents almost touching the spruce. The cleared space between them and the shack was littered with lumber, wire cable, oil drums, air hose and tools. The new headframe rose starkly above the shaft. The tugger, the miner's term for the small and powerful air-driven hoist, lay black and silent under the raw lumber of its three-sided shelter, waiting for the compressor.

As Tully and Bill stepped into the clearing, Tully whistled shrilly and waved to Alec who sat in the cat seat, a cold cigar in his mouth, letting the silence and the stillness flow over him. He waved lazily, then heaved himself to his feet and swung down. The orange-painted compressor lashed with chains to the bed of the trailer behind him was the last of the heavy machinery to be hauled.

Approaching, Tully asked, "How's the big city, boy?"

Alec grinned in reply, settled down on his heels in the shade of the cat and said, "I had to leave. The night life was killing me." He touched a match to his dead cigar. "I saw Kevin from seven to seven-thirty last night and staggered off to bed."

Standing by the compressor, Tully shrugged into his shirt, looking approvingly at the way Alec had lashed down this piece of equipment for its rough ride. He hunkered down beside Alec while Bill Ligon, unbidden, began lugging up the heavy planks on which they would manhandle the compressor to the ground.

Tully lighted a cigarette and asked, "Kevin all right?"

"Sure. He wants to come out."

"Tell him to wait until we get squared around," Tully said. "Tomorrow we'll hook up the tugger and get to work underground. You spot the places on the grade that need shooting and when you're ready we'll pull the compressor off."

"Man, that compressor won't be cool for a whole year," Alec said.

"That's the idea." Tully flipped his cigarette away. "Well, let's unload it." He came to his feet and then Alec rose wearily. They unlashed the chains, then Tully swung up into the trailer along with Bill and Alec. They maneuvered the heavy machine onto the planks, and then with Tully heaving and the other two braking the heavy machine, they eased it down the planks to the ground.

Finished, they leaned on a machine, catching their wind,

and now Tully examined the compressor. It was a type familiar to him, rugged and almost new. When the five barrels of gas had been unloaded from the trailer and hoisted to timber trestles in the shade of the spruce, Tully tramped back to the compressor. Bill Ligon set off into the timber to finish laying pipe while Alec trailed after Tully.

"Let's wind her up and see what parts shook loose," Tully said. "How's the gas?"

"Didn't check."

Tully reached over and removed the cap; stuck his finger in the tank and felt the cool gasoline almost even with the cap rim. At the same time, he noticed fine white crystals scattered thinly in the oil smudge around the tank's opening. For a puzzled moment he wondered what sort of antiknock compound the owner had been mixing with his gasoline. On impulse then he licked his finger and touched it to the crystals, then put his finger to his mouth. He was expecting to taste and identify some chemical. The taste of the crystals, however, was sweet.

Baffled, he repeated the act, and then it came to him with a crashing abruptness that this was sugar.

"Alec!" he called angrily. "Come here!"

When Alec came over, Tully pointed to the crystals, and said, "Taste that." Alec, like Tully, wet his finger, tasted the crystals and then raised his glance to Tully.

"That's sugar."

"Catch on?" Tully asked grimly.

Suddenly, Alec began to swear furiously. They both knew that if the compressor, with its fuel containing sugar, were started, it would only be a matter of moments before the engine was hopelessly fouled. As soon as the gas achieved combustion, the sugar would burn and freeze the pistons to the cylinder walls. A total engine overhaul would be necessary to put the compressor again in operation.

Tully knew also that this was not accidental. Whoever had smashed the fuel pump had poured sugar into the gasoline. He knew that Alec knew this too.

There was real misery in Alec's dark eyes now. "I swear I

don't know how it could have happened, Tully. I picked up the compressor as soon as I got in and parked the trailer right by my window last night."

"Did you run it?"

Alec shook his head. "I never even tried to turn it over."

For a bleak minute Tully regarded the compressor. At that moment he hated it, knowing that this was unreasonable, yet it stood as a symbol of their frustration and helplessness. If he had not been curious about the crystals and tasted them, they would have started the motor and again been delayed for a week.

He was aware that Alec was looking at him, waiting for him to speak. He sighed, and then swore softly.

"Forget it, boy. You can't sleep on every piece of equipment we pick up. It's just that we've got to watch every piece of machinery from now on to see if it's been tampered with."

Again he looked at the compressor, calculating what would have to be done. The tank must be removed, drained and carefully cleaned of the syrup it contained. To do the job really well, a section of the tank would have to be cut out with an acetylene torch, the interior thoroughly scrubbed, and the section welded back.

Grimly he said, "Well, let's take the tank off, Alec."

"They're a hell of a job to clean," Alec said gloomily. Tully told him then that he would take it back to Azurite this afternoon.

"You want me to take it in?"

Tully thought a moment. "No, I want you on the road tomorrow. I'll take it in tonight and be back by tomorrow morning, I hope."

As the sun heeled over further, Tully and Alec got the tank off the compressor and loaded it in the back of Alec's jeep. Tully left instructions on tomorrow's work for the crew, then shrugged into a greasy denim jacket, climbed into the jeep and set off down Alec's bushwhack trail for Azurite. The first two miles of road through pushed-over timber, rock face, bog and crushed windfalls were unbelievably rough and almost succeeded in stalling the jeep. Afterwards, when he had picked up the grade stakes on Alec's pioneer road, the going was easier and Tully relaxed a little.

He had not realized how tired he was and what a strain these three driving days of getting started had been. He reviewed them now in his own mind. For one thing, the weather had been on his side. All the heavy equipment which rain could have stalled was at the mine location. Secondly, he had a hard-working, experienced crew who did not need to be driven. Third, the crew and machinery were under shelter and they could begin mining as soon as the compressor was repaired. The long, costly job of building the road did not bother him so long as they were getting ore out of the ground.

But memory of sabotage to the compressor, coupled with the damaging of the cat, galled him. It had already accounted for two full days' delay, and there was no anticipating where trouble would crop up again, since someone (and without any proof, he suspected Ben Hodes) was sharpshooting for them.

Dusk began to steal into the timber, and the fresh smell of raw earth on the newly bulldozed road was pleasant to Tully. But it held a reminder that when bad weather broke this road would be a bog until freeze-up.

When the lights of town became visible, Tully felt a faint pleasure stirring within. The reason for it was simple enough: there was an evening with Sarah ahead of him. It was too late to get into a machine shop, so he would head for the hotel, call Sarah, clean up and have dinner in the evening with her.

As he turned into the business section of town he observed the unaccustomed traffic, and for an amazed moment he wondered what had happened. Jeeps and pickup trucks stood parked rank upon rank along the main street. It was only when he caught sight of a pair of men coming out of the hotel dressed in red caps and jackets that he remembered hunting season would open day after tomorrow. Remembering Kevin's admonition to hire only men who would stick during hunting season, he wondered if his crew would be full strength tomorrow. As he pulled up in front of the hotel, he made a mental note to buy some red shirts for his men in the morning, since to some hunters anything that moved or made a sound in the timber was fair game.

He remembered another thing now too; all unguarded Sarah Moffit property and machinery was liable to tampering, and he took the keys out of the jeep, lifted out the tank and shouldered his way into a lobby crowded with hunters. The clerk was not to be seen and Tully labored through the lobby and up the stairs with his burden, deposited them in his room and then came down to the lobby phone booth. Calling the Moffit apartment, he was answered by Mrs. Moffit.

"This is Tully, Mrs. Moffit. How are you?"

"When did you get back, Tully? I thought you were there until you ran out of grub."

"I got hungry for a look at a pretty girl," Tully said. "Have you got one around?"

Mrs. Moffit laughed. "Not at the moment. Sarah's having dinner with Beth Hodes at the Kellys'. I think they're coming over here afterwards. Sarah's got some new records."

Tully felt a sharp disappointment, but he said, "Mind if I listen to them too?"

"Don't be silly. Come when you're ready."

Tully hung up and stepped into the lobby, heading for the stairs. The clerk behind the desk now called to him. "Say, you ever get that call?"

Tully halted. "What call?"

"From San Diego." The clerk reached over to a pad, consulted it and said, "You're to call San Diego, operator 209. She's tried five times to get you today."

"Thanks," Tully said. Climbing the stairs, he wondered who would be calling him from San Diego, and he smiled at his own curiosity. He knew a hundred men in the Naval hospital there, and perhaps twenty of them plus several of the staff who were his friends knew he'd been planning to spend some time here in the mountains. Probably it was some sort of celebration like a promotion, a discharge or an affirmative verdict on a total disability examination. He would shower and dress and put in his call from the restaurant downstreet.

Twenty minutes later, shaven, bathed, and with a solid belt of bourbon in him, Tully stepped into the restaurant. Most of the late-dinner hunters had cleared out, but some still sat on the counter stools. Tully, on his way to the phone booth in the rear, left his order, asked for and received a handful of change and went to the phone booth.

He had a minute's wait before San Diego answered and in another half minute he heard a voice that was instantly familiar and welcome. It was Doc Byrnes—Lieutenant Commander Eugene P. Byrnes—and his booming voice, earshattering over a thousand miles of telephone wire, was warm and raucous.

"Tully, you son of a gun. I've been trying to get you ever since I heard the news."

"Hi, Doc," Tully said. "What's with you and your butcher shop?"

"Never better, son. How about that big news, huh?"

Tully frowned into the mouthpiece. "What news is this, Doc?"

"Don't go coy on me, boy. You damn well know what it is. Your new job, what else?"

"Oh!" For a moment Tully was bewildered. "Oh, yeah, I do have a new one. How did you know about it though?"

"It's a long story, and a crazy coincidence. This noon I was eating at the Commissary with your favorite redhead from Records. Remember her name?"

"Dottie Humphreys? How could I forget her?"

Byrnes's raucous laughter almost rang through the restaurant. Then he continued. "Well, she got a call today from the secretary of your employer."

"Just a minute," Tully cut in. "Who is my new employer?"

"It's me you're asking?" Byrnes demanded. "Don't you know who you're working for?"

"No. You tell me."

"Dottie said it was the Sarah Moffit Mine, Incorporated."

"That's right, go on," Tully said gently.

"Go on where? I only wanted to congratulate you."

"Thanks. But get back to Dottie Humphreys. The secretary of the Sarah Moffit Mine called her. What for?"

"Oh, the usual personnel check-up, I suppose. This dame told Dottie they wanted to clear you quickly so they could put you to work. They wanted a short medical history and a short fill-in on your military service. She even wanted confirmation that you'd received the Navy Cross. What are they hiring out there—only certified heroes?"

Tully's bewilderment was not complete. There was no president of the Sarah Moffit Mine, nor did the nonexistent president have a secretary, yet a call had been made.

"Hello, hello, you still on?" Byrnes roared.

"Sure, Doc, I'm just a little confused is all."

"Well, it's a job, isn't it? What kind of a job by the way?"

Tully saw no reason for not stringing along with his friend, so he said, "It's a good one, Doc. I'll be a guaranteed millionaire in three months and five days."

"You lucky hound," Byrnes roared. "Here I am in this uniform while half the babies in Cincinnati are being born without me."

"You've got all the stuff there for a self-inflicted wound," Tully said. "Why don't you use it?"

"It's against our union rule," Byrnes said, and laughed. Then his voice suddenly became serious. "How's it going, kid—the legs, I mean? Any recurrences?"

"Some," Tully said. "It doesn't bother me any."

"Great. Well, the whole gang said to give you their congratulations. They also asked if you'd lay aside a block of stock for them."

"I'll air-mail it tomorrow," Tully said.

There was another minute of talk about mutual friends, and then Doc Byrnes rang off. Slowly Tully hung up the receiver and tramped back to the booth where his dinner was waiting. He sat down and stared absently at his food, and his appetite was gone. It was plain that Sarah, lying like a cunning child, was checking up on him.

Does she know? he thought glumly. Had Sarah stumbled onto his swindle? For a bitter moment Tully considered this carefully. Reviewing what he had done that might have given him away, he could think of nothing.

Then maybe Sarah's call was a routine character check. The more Tully thought about this, the more reasonable it seemed—and galling. But after all, neither Kevin nor Sarah knew any more about him than was told in the forged letters from Jimmy. It was only natural that they check on him—Kevin because Tully was his partner, and Sarah because she was protecting Kevin.

Still, it was bitter to think that Sarah had done this behind his back. She had lied shamelessly in order to get doubts returned, and he stared glumly at his food and then listlessly began to push it around his plate.

He wondered dismally what his safest move was now, or even if he should move at all. Sarah would never know that Doc Byrnes had given him this information. Whatever facts she had learned about Tully merely confirmed what he had told her about himself. Instead of confronting her with evidence of her deceit and suspicion, maybe he should ignore the whole affair. He suddenly decided not to mention it to Sarah, but deep within him a warning voice told him, *Just be careful—be damn careful.*

Later, as he was mounting the stairs to the Moffit apartment, he heard music and halted. A combo was playing "Sweet Georgia Brown." As soon as he had identified the piano player as Dave Brubeck, he went up and knocked at the door. Sarah let him in.

She was dressed in green velvet slacks and a pink pearl-studded cashmere coat sweater. She looked beautiful, Tully thought, as he smiled and tried to make his greeting seem normal and offhand. "This the new music?" he asked, tipping his head toward the phonograph.

Sarah said it was, and as Tully walked into the room he said hello to Mrs. Moffit who was knitting on the sofa and to

Beth Hodes who was seated on the floor by the phonograph, sorting out records.

Beth turned down the volume a little and then looked frankly at him. "Last time I saw you—no, the only time—you looked like a tiger ready to pounce."

Tully grinned. "That's my Elks Club expression."

Beth smiled, too. "I like this one better."

Sarah came over and sat on the arm of the sofa as Tully slacked into a chair. While the record finished he watched her closely, looking for any change in her manner. She was whistling thinly and expertly a counterpoint to Brubeck's piano, and to Tully it seemed as if there was nothing on her mind except the enjoyment of the music. When the record ended, Sarah glanced over at him. "What's new at the mine, Tully?"

Tully hesitated a moment, wondering if Beth Hodes should hear this, and he decided it didn't matter. "The Little People took another crack at us," Tully said wryly. "Somebody put sugar in the compressor gas tank."

"Somebody what?" Sarah asked blankly.

Tully told her of his discovery while unloading the compressor, and explained what it would have done to the engine, adding that this was the reason why he was in town instead of at the mine.

Beth listened with interest, but when Tully looked at her she dropped her glance to the pile of records before her. *She suspects Ben, too,* Tully thought.

Mrs. Moffit observed, "Someone has a very strange sense of humor."

"Tut-tut, Ma," Sarah said, almost angrily. "You mustn't be too harsh on your favorite prankster."

Mrs. Moffit looked up in surprise. "Well, I declare, you sound angry, Sarah."

"Sense of humor she says," Sarah said in angry mockery. "There's no humor in it, Ma! Whoever's doing this is plenty serious. The harder we work, the more of it there'll be, too."

Mrs. Moffit looked at Tully. "Do you think that, Tully?"

"I suppose I do, Mrs. Moffit."

"You mean there's somebody doesn't want you to get the mine operating?"

Tully only nodded. Mrs. Moffit looked from Tully to Sarah. "Now, who would wish that sort of bad luck on anyone?"

Sarah refrained from answering. Beth Hodes was leafing through a stack of albums as if she had not heard. Tully said nothing.

Sarah said, breaking the silence, "Put on some Errol Garner, Beth."

"Just one more and then I'll have to go," Beth said.

"It's early," Sarah protested.

"And I'm tired." Beth put on the Garner record. They listened in silence. Afterwards Beth rose. Tully rose, too. "I'll take you home, Beth."

"Oh, don't bother," Beth said.

"Yes, do bother," Sarah countered. "She's moved out of their house, you know, Tully. Ben's watching her every minute. I think you'd better go with her." Tully helped Beth with her coat and while Beth was saying good night to Mrs. Moffit, Tully was waiting for Sarah to ask him to return after he dropped Beth off. There was no invitation forthcoming, not even after he said good night to Mrs. Moffit.

When the door closed behind him, the old fears returned. *She knows,* Tully thought. *Here's where the deep freeze starts.*

Tully and Beth walked downstreet to the jeep parked in front of the hotel, and then Tully drove Beth home. The Kelly house was a small white frame affair, neat as only the widow of a Welsh miner could keep it. No lights were showing.

Beth, climbing out of the jeep, said, "Don't bother to come up, Tully. Good night."

Tully, however, swung out of the jeep and started up the dark walk toward the house. It was dark inside, so Tully had almost reached the steps before he saw the black hulk before him. A split second later Beth gave a start, and then halted, too.

"Is it you, Ben?" Beth asked.

"I want to talk with you, Beth." Ben Hodes's voice was heavy, serious and almost threatening.

Tully said quickly, "You want to talk with him, Beth?"

"No."

To Ben, Tully said, "Then step aside while I escort the lady to the door."

"I mean it, Beth. I want to talk with you."

"Not tonight, Ben. You come down to the office tomorrow and I'll talk with you as long as you want."

There was a moment of silence in which none of them moved, and then Tully put a foot on the bottom step. "Let's call it an evening," he suggested mildly. He reached back for Beth's arm and drew her close to him, and then mounted the steps, prepared to shoulder Ben aside and to accept whatever followed.

Surprisingly, Ben stepped back and let them by him. Tully waited until Beth had unlocked the door, bidden him good night and closed it, and then he turned, standing on the balls of his feet waiting for Ben to make his move. When Ben turned and tramped down the steps, Tully breathed a sigh of relief and followed him.

"Want a ride?" Tully asked.

He saw Ben's shoulders lift in a shrug, and then Ben said gloomily, "Why not?"

Tully waited to speak until the jeep was in motion, and then he said, "Well, it didn't work, Ben."

Hodes looked at him. "What didn't work?"

"The sugar in the compressor tank."

Hodes was silent a bare second. "What are you talking about, man?"

Tully said, "When I catch your man, I don't think he'll want to work for you again."

"Now what does that mean?" Hodes asked, a faint amusement in his heavy voice.

"It means I'll send him back to you in a basket."

He could hear Ben's snort above the sound of the motor.

"It's got to be bigger than these fleabites, Ben, to do me any harm, but when it does I'm coming after you."

"I'm slow," Ben said, almost plaintively. "Dumb it up. What are you talking about?"

Tully glanced at him. "I've got one hundred and twenty days to pay back a ten-thousand-dollar loan. If anybody gets in the way of my paying it, he'll get fitted for new teeth, and that's a promise."

"One hundred and twenty days," Ben said dreamily. "On the one hundred and twenty-first day I'll have your half of the Sarah Moffit in court." He looked at Tully. "I'll have all my teeth, too. I'll even have something else." Tully said nothing, and Ben went on. "I'll have your hide nailed to the wall, friend Gibbs."

Tully said mildly, "Where you going?"

"Elks."

They did not speak until Tully deposited him before the Elks building. Ben courteously thanked him, bidding good night, and Tully drove off down the street.

Next morning Tully cleaned out the compressor tank at one of the garages, and afterwards stopped at the town's lone clothing store and bought a half-dozen cheap scarlet shirts. At the *Nugget* office he bought some cardboard "No Hunting Allowed" signs and by midmorning he was on his way back to the mine.

It was a beautiful, crisp fall day, and Tully almost wished he were hunting too. When he came to the new road he saw that several vehicles had passed over his last night's tracks. Beyond the climb to the first ridge, he could see where two camps had been set up by hunters in the scattered spruce in preparation for opening day of hunting season tomorrow. At the first camp, three men were erecting a tent. As he neared, one of the men, a stocky, soft man, wearing rimless glasses and a friendly expression, flagged him down. Tully braked the jeep to a stop and wondered idly as the man approached why most men looked more absurd in caps, especially red ones, than they did in hats.

The man put his hand on the windshield frame, said, "Hi," and then asked the inevitable question. "Where's a good place for elk around here?"

Tully said, "I'm a stranger here myself. Five or six miles north though there's a mine working. They're pretty noisy, so I'd stay away from that area."

The hunter thanked him and Tully drove on. The second camp was shipshape but deserted, and Tully supposed the members of this party were out spotting likely-looking country for tomorrow's hunt.

As he drove on, his thoughts returned to last night and Sarah. If he were the brooding kind, he thought, now would be the time to brood. Even if he hadn't known of Sarah's call to San Diego, he would have thought her actions last night almost unfriendly. The hour Beth had chosen to go home had been early. The natural, friendly thing for Sarah to have done would have been to invite him back for a drink and more music. Mrs. Moffit could gracefully have retired and if Sarah had wanted they could have had a pleasant evening. *I've probably had my last one with her.*

Still, her sudden coolness didn't make sense. She had learned nothing from her San Diego call that didn't jibe with what he had already told her. Tully guessed shrewdly that a normal person, when his suspicions turned out to be unfounded, was apt to be overcordial to the person suspected. Sarah had been anything but overcordial to him. That meant she still suspected him on other grounds, but what were they? Even if Dottie Humphreys had been flip and had seemed too familiar with Tully's service and medical history, this was scarcely grounds for Sarah's treatment of him. It was something else, something unguessable.

But Tully felt a bitter regret at Sarah's change of manner toward him. He admitted to himself now that she was already a large part of his new life. Up until yesterday he had had the hope, naïve as it was, that Sarah would never know of his scheming and his dishonesty. But somehow, perhaps intuitively, she had sensed his deception and was beginning to back off. Would Kevin do the same? In a few weeks, would he be just another date for Sarah, to be treated like any personable young man with a known character weakness—just a guy to kill time with? And would Kevin begin to mistrust both his judgment and his work? He did not know, but he had the uneasy and unpleasant feeling that command of the situation was slipping away from him.

The jeep had now reached the end of the surveyed road. Tully halted it, climbed out and tacked a "No Hunting" sign on a prominent tree close by. Then he turned off on the wretched bushwhack road. Where the timber began to thicken Tully shifted into low low and picked up speed for the turn and the steep grade beyond. As he made the turn, wheels churning, he suddenly jammed on his brakes. There ahead of him up the hill in the narrow lane was a stalled pickup truck. Already its wheels were mired in the loose earth churned up by the cat.

Swearing under his breath, Tully cut the motor. Three sweating, unshaven, red-jacketed hunters who had been trying to heave out the truck straightened up and looked at him. Two of them, Tully saw, were already a little drunk. A long-legged, square-jawed character, a dead cigar clamped in his mouth, came stumbling down the hill in the loose dirt toward the jeep. He hauled up alongside Tully, his chest heaving. Tully could smell the rank odor of long-drunk whiskey on his breath. "Say, you mind giving us a hand so we can get up this hill?" the hunter asked.

"I don't mind giving you a hand, but you're not going up the hill," Tully said quietly. "You're going down."

The man looked carefully at him, and then said, "Who says we are?"

"I do."

"This is forest land and we'll go any damn place we please on it, Buster," the man said flatly.

"You're on a private road on a working mining claim," Tully contradicted him. "You're getting off, too."

The man looked at him dubiously. "You wouldn't be kidding me, would you?"

Tully tilted his head. "Go back down the road a piece and

you'll find a sign that says 'Private Property, No Trespassing Allowed.' "

"I didn't see it."

"I can't blame you for that. I just put it up. Still, it's there and it means what it says." He gestured toward the truck. "This is the only access road to the mine and you're blocking it. Even if you climbed this hill, you'd be bogged down for a week in the stuff ahead, so you'd better back down."

The hunter stared rebelliously at Tully for a long moment, then turned his head and called, "Hey, Joe, come here."

Both Joe and his companion came lurching down the slope to join the long-legged man who said, when they halted beside him, "This guy says he owns this land and we're to get the hell off."

One of his short, heavyset companions snorted, "Ha! Let him get us off."

"I'll get you off," Tully said levelly. "If you'll listen, you can hear a bulldozer working up on top. If you aren't cleared off of here in an hour, I'll bring it down and turn your damn truck upside down and then run over it."

The short man said, "Real tough, huh?"

"All you've got to do to find out is stay here."

The third man said belligerently, "Why don't you post your land then?"

Tully took a No Trespassing card from the seat, stepped out and impaled it on the broken branch of a spruce nearby. He turned and said, "All right, it's posted."

The long-legged man said, "Where's your boundary?"

"Right where the No Trespassing sign is back there."

"Okay, let's leave the jerk alone," the stocky man said to his companions. The three of them turned without another word and struggled back up the hill. Tully climbed in and started the jeep and backed around the curve and out onto the timber flats. Switching off the engine, he drew out a cigarette, lit it and then leaned back and listened to the truck driver frantically gunning his motor in an effort to back the truck down the slope. It took a solid half hour of brush-laying, alternating with a furious gunning of the motor, before the truck backed into sight from out of the spruce. The three men pushing were now drenched with sweat and filthy from the churned dirt of the slope. As the truck backed off the road they stumbled wearily in its wake, then turned to glare at Tully. He started his motor and swung onto the road.

"Wise guy," the taller man growled as Tully passed him.

In another ten minutes Tully achieved camp. Minutes afterwards he and Alec were busy installing the tank and the incident with the hunters was forgotten. By midafternoon they had the compressor spotted and working. There was some rock to shoot at the top of the ridge before Alec could start bulldozing the grade. By late afternoon the noise of the jackhammer was filling the forest with its working din.

That night after supper Tully maneuvered the jeep down so that its headlamps could give him light to work by, and he ran the jackhammer until he had to knock off the noise and let his crew sleep.

He was awakened at bare dawn by the first chorus of shots from the hunters celebrating opening day. After breakfast in the mess tent, he distributed the red shirts to his crew. Charlie Short, a stubby, wide-chested Welshman, picked up the shirt from the board mess table and said, "You figure they'll be shooting down the shaft, Tully?"

"Yes," Bill Ligon said promptly. "Three years ago I was working at Phil Miller's gas station on Main Street. Damned if some hunter didn't put a slug into the gas pump. It was painted red, too."

As the crew changed into their red shirts they began swapping hunting stories, commenting on the dryness of the weather and the likelihood of a small kill. Tully knew every man loved to hunt, and he decided that the first day it rained or snowed he would give them a day off to bring in some meat.

As Tully stepped out into the chill early morning, he halted and cocked his head listening. From all directions, but especially from the west there was the distant sound of shooting. It was as if a small guerrilla war were being waged in these mountains. Alec stepped up beside him, borrowed a cigarette and listened too.

"Does that racket make you want to be out there?" Tully asked Alec.

Alec shook his head in negation. "Not me. I eat elk every year, a bull, but I don't get one while half of Texas is shooting at me."

Tully grinned and they both started for the bulldozer. The crew had already scattered to their various jobs. Suddenly, there was a clanging of steel on the bulldozer, and then the unmistakable sound of a ricochet bullet followed by the sharp report of a rifle from a distant ridge several hundred yards away. Alec swore wildly, then turned and faced the ridge, waving his red shirt. A second later dust suddenly geysered up between Alec and the tent, and there came another sharp report.

"He's shooting at you!" Tully shouted. He grabbed Alec's arm and whirled him around, pointing toward the 'dozer. They both ran for cover as a third searching shot smashed into an empty oil drum beside the mess tent.

Tully and Alec hit the dirt at the same time in the shelter of the cat's tread.

"Is that guy crazy?" Alec asked wrathfully. "What the hell is he doing?" As if in answer the distant rifleman shot again. There was the clang of a bullet on the 'dozer motor and the following clap of the rifle. Still another shot at the 'dozer followed. Both Tully and Alec, lying flat on the dirt, waited, looking at each other with a wild bitterness in their eyes.

Suddenly the rifleman shifted to another target, this time the tugger. He put six shots into the shaft and tugger as Tully watched wrathfully. Then as if to keep them down, he switched again to the 'dozer, putting several more shots into it. His aim shifted then to the distant compressor, and Tully groaned as he heard the slugs reach home.

For twenty minutes they lay in the dirt while all the machinery in sight, plus air hoses and gas tanks, were thoroughly worked over. Lying there, a murdering wrath within him, Tully counted at least forty shots.

As abruptly as the shooting began, it now ended. Tully and Alec waited a minute, then Tully rose and dashed for the mess tent, Alec on his heels. The cook had taken to the timber, but his rifle stood in the corner of the tent. Tully grasped it and lunged outside and raced for the timber. He heard Alec running behind him, and then Alec grabbed his arm and halted him. "I'm going to hunt that guy down and kill him," Tully said thinly. "Let go!"

"Don't be a sucker," Alec said. "Hell, an Indian couldn't track him on that ridge rock. Besides that, the timber is full of hunters. How you going to tell which one did it?"

Beyond his wrath, Tully knew Alec was right, and he slowly relaxed, his anger unfading. It could have been one of the angry drunk hunters he had booted off the property yesterday, or it could be Hodes's man who had instructions to shoot up the camp and then lose himself in the anonymity of half a hundred hunters.

6

Tully's first move was to plug the holes in the gas drums lest the cascading gasoline catch fire from the cookshack stove. Alec went directly to the cat to assess the damage. Tully, however, was more concerned with the compressor, and he went back to examine it thoroughly. Outside of a hole in the gas tank it was unharmed, but the cat was another matter. Its radiator was riddled; its new fuel pump was smashed, but the block was undamaged. The squat tugger was unharmed, but the air hose was holed. Estimating what the hidden rifleman had accomplished, Tully guessed that it would be a week before parts could be obtained from Denver and the cat made usable again. A simple welding job would put the compressor in use by tomorrow.

Tully looked up to see the cook cautiously entering the clearing. He tramped slowly over to Tully and halted. "You never hired me for this," he said flatly. "I quit."

"All right," Tully said resignedly. "Get your stuff together. I'm going to town."

The rest of the crew, pair by pair, drifted into camp, drawn from their work by the clanging of the rifle slugs on metal. Since they had not been under fire, they were less disturbed than the cook, and Tully, explaining it as retaliation from the hunters he had kicked off the claim yesterday, sent them back to work. Afterwards he and Alec repeated their yesterday's chore of removing the gas tank from the compressor. An hour later Tully was again on his way to town.

He ignored the cook beside him as he considered what he must do next. First, he would check the camp of the hunters he had booted off the claim the day before. He was certain that if one of them was the rifleman, his guilt would show. If he was satisfied that the hunters were innocent, that left Hodes, and he would have his showdown with Ben Hodes.

After a bruising ride down to the survey road, he came alert, watching the dust of the road for the story told by the tire tracks of the pickup. The truck, oddly, had kept to the road as if the hunters had abandoned the idea of making camp on the mine property. When he came to the second hunters' camp he stopped the jeep, hoping someone there could give him news of the pickup and its occupants. However, the camp was deserted. Driving on, he noted that the tire tracks of the pickup still clung to the road and were made yesterday. They were still there as he pulled off the mine road onto the access road.

Reluctantly, Tully decided that the hunters were not guilty. Discouraged by his ordering them off, they had apparently chosen to camp in another part of the county. It seemed unlikely that one of their number had been the rifleman. If they were interested enough in finding likely hunting country, then an elk kill was more important to them than this hoodlum retaliation.

That left Ben Hodes. At the Liberty Gulch road Tully turned right toward the Mahaffey. Approaching the mill, he noted the half-dozen cars parked by the mill office. He did not know what sort of car Ben Hodes drove, but he was certain that it would not be one of the old model cars on the lot. Swinging into the parking lot, he stopped the jeep, climbed out and entered the Mahaffey office. Two middle-aged women, one seated at a typewriter, the other standing before a file cabinet, looked around as he entered.

"I'm looking for Mr. Hodes," Tully announced.

The file clerk said, "He's not in and he won't be for a week. He's at the mining convention in Denver."

Tully scowled. "When did he leave?"

"Yesterday morning."

For an angry moment Tully considered this. There was every reason in the world for Ben to be absent now, he thought grimly. The mining convention was the most reasonable of excuses to avoid the consequences of the shooting. Ben could easily have arranged for the events of this morning, then have left town to ensure the appearance of his own innocence.

Wordlessly, angrily, Tully wheeled and went out. On the drive back to town he made a bleak appraisal of the future. What had once been only a nuisance had now turned into a genuine threat. He had promised Ben Hodes that when it did, Hodes would be in real trouble. Yet Ben was unreachable. When he returned he would blandly protest his innocence, ask for proof of his guilt and continue to sabotage the Sarah Moffit operations. *No he won't,* Tully thought grimly.

When he reached town, he delivered the cook at the nearest bar, unloaded the compressor tank to be patched, then headed straight for the courthouse. On the second floor he found Sheriff Olson in his musty office that smelled of floor-cleaning compound and, oddly, of freshly watered plants. A row of enormous potted geraniums filled both high windows of the otherwise drab room.

Sheriff Olson was seated in a swivel chair facing a scarred rolltop desk and he was carefully reading a tattered Montgomery Ward catalogue when Tully entered. He was a small, bald, wiry man, in his early sixties, dressed in tight-fitting Oregon-style pants and blue denim shirt. A curl-brim Stetson lay on the desk. But instead of completing his costume and wearing cowman's boots, he wore bulbous-toed high lace shoes.

Sheriff Olson had a lean, amiable face, bisected by one of the most untidy bale-of-hay, roan-colored mustaches that Tully had ever seen; it was as if he had modeled himself, not quite successfully, after a picture of a paterfamilias of seventy-five years ago.

He looked at Tully with total friendliness as he closed the catalogue and dropped it to the desk.

"Hi, young feller," he said, his voice friendly. "Looking for me?"

Listen to the rube accent, Tully thought, and he was sure the sheriff was living up to his own conception of a long-gone, gun-toting, tobacco-chewing, rough-diamond sheriff of western fiction.

"I guess I am," Tully said. "How do you go about swearing out a peace bond against somebody?"

The sheriff's bushy eyebrows raised. He looked searchingly at Tully as he fished in his shirt pocket and drew out an old curve-stem pipe. He made no effort to load it or light it, but put it in his mouth and talked around it. "Why," he said slowly, judiciously, "you go to the justice court, state your case with your witnesses, then if the justice court grants a peace bond, the constable hauls your man in and he pays up."

"Not you?"

Sheriff Olson's mustache lifted faintly as he smiled. "Well, we got no constable here for the justice court, so I guess I'm your man. It's illegal, but I'm still your man." He paused. "Who you gunning for?"

"Ben Hodes," Tully said grimly. "Where's the justice court?"

Sheriff Olson leaned back in his chair and ignored Tully's question. "Ben Hodes, huh? It don't seem likely. What'd he do?"

"Somebody he hired shot up my camp today. He wrecked my machinery so it'll be out of commission for a week. Once I get it repaired, he'll do it again." Tully paused to isolate this. "But mostly I don't like people shooting at me and my men whenever they like, and I want him bonded. If that doesn't work, I'm going to start shooting back."

Sheriff Olson ignored this also. "What proof you got Ben Hodes hired a man to shoot you up?"

"Without going into a thirty-minute lecture, I'll tell you this much," Tully said. "Hodes has been trying for years to buy the Vicksburg Claims for a tenth of what they're worth. I've got them and I'm mining them. I think Hodes doesn't want me to, and this is his way of trying to scare me off."

Sheriff Olson said nothing and there was a long silence. Finally Tully said, "Well?"

"I'm still waiting for your proof," Sheriff Olson said.

Tully tipped his head toward the street. "Would a shot-up compressor gas tank impress you?"

"No, no," Olson said, still amiably. "I don't doubt you were shot at. But what proof you got that Hodes is behind it?"

"Who else could be?" Tully countered.

"It's hunting season," Olson said mildly. "These hunters nowadays will shoot at anything, including their wives." He cackled at his own humor, but Tully did not even smile.

"It's hard to mistake a bulldozer for an elk, or even for your wife."

"You've never seen mine," Olson said, and cackled again.

Unsmilingly Tully waited for his laughter to ebb, then he said, "Well?"

"I'm still waiting for proof," Olson said. His voice remained friendly.

"Look," Tully said, anger pushing him. "As a resident of this county and a property owner, I'm entitled to the protection of the law against people who're endangering my life and my property. What are you going to do about it?"

Olson shrugged. "What can I? You want me to round up every hunter in the country and ask him if he shot at a bulldozer by mistake?"

"That might be a start," Tully observed angrily.

Now some of the amiability left the sheriff's eyes. He removed the pipe from his mouth and pointed the stem at Tully. "Don't go telling me my business, young feller. I'll be glad to take you to our J.P. when you show me proof that Ben Hodes shot at you. Until you can, you better keep a civil tongue in your face."

Tully checked his anger and said reasonably, "Sheriff, I counted forty shots that were fired at our camp. Those shots were not aimed at people, they were aimed at our machinery —our cat, our compressor, our tugger and our fuel. What does that sound like to you?"

"Like a lot of shooting," Olson said, and cackled again.

Tully thought suddenly, *Why I'm dealing with an idiot.* But he went on, "Does that sound like a nearsighted hunter?"

Olson shook his head in negation.

"Then it could only have been someone interested in stopping our operations. Do you agree?"

Sheriff Oslon nodded his head in affirmation.

"Since Hodes is the only man interested in halting our operations, then isn't it logical that he hired the rifleman?"

"Nope," Sheriff Olson said. "It isn't logical unless you got proof."

Tully stood looking at him a long moment, then he said, "Oh, the hell with it," turned and walked out of the office. The full tide of his anger almost sickened him as he tramped down the stairs and halted in the corridor.

He might as well face the fact now that he was as much in Indian country as the first settler in the West. This was Ben Hodes's town and those were Ben Hodes's people and he, Tully Gibbs, was the foreigner. Without framing it in his own mind he knew that if he retaliated against Hodes with Hodes's weapons, he would be in immediate and deep trouble. His anger still riding him, he moved into the cross corridor heading for the clerk's office and Sarah.

When he entered, Sarah was busy selling a license to the owner of a new car, and she greeted him perfunctorily. He took one of the high stools in the far corner of the room and lighted a cigarette. Presently Justin Byers came out of the vault carrying a big ledger which he put on the counter and studied a moment. Then he returned the ledger to the vault, came out, saw Tully, nodded in greeting, picked up his hat which was lying on the corner of the counter and left the room. Soon Sarah was finished with the license registration and came over.

When, ten minutes later and still hunched on the bookkeeper's stool, Tully finished telling her of the shooting, he felt the first edge of his anger gone. Sarah was seated at her typing desk, half turned away from it, and she heard him out in silence. Then she smiled almost wryly and stubbed out her cigarette in the ashtray. "But Olson's right, Tully," she said finally. "You do need proof."

Tully groaned. "There's that word again."

"All the same, you haven't a shred of evidence."

Tully slid off the stool, rammed his hands in his pockets and stood looking down at her. "So we get it fixed, so he shoots it up again, so we get it fixed and he does it still again?"

"Oh, I know, Tully," Sarah said. There was genuine sympathy in her voice that almost surprised Tully. They looked in each other's eyes for a wordless moment.

Tully said gloomily, "What would happen if I shot up the Mahaffey?"

"You'd be jailed."

"Yeah, but I can play rough, too," Tully said grimly. "It's easy enough to slip a handful of dynamite caps in the stuff the Mahaffey's milling."

"You'd just hurt the workmen."

"He wasn't worried about hurting mine."

"You don't mean that, Tully," Sarah said softly.

Tully sighed. "No, I guess I don't. Only this guy has got to be stopped. I think it's time for me to take him apart. All I'll get out of that is a fine at the most." He looked at Sarah. "Maybe if I do it three or four times, he'll get the idea."

Sarah said nothing, and Tully grinned crookedly. "The trouble is he's not here to take apart. He likely won't be for two weeks. Anything can happen in that time."

Sarah was silent a long moment, and then she said, "The only thing we can do, Tully, is to try and stop it. Have you thought of asking Olson to be deputized?"

"Ha!" Tully said scornfully. "Olson can't wait to do me a big fat favor."

"Not you. He wouldn't think of it, but every man you've got working for you out there has grown up in this town. If they say they're in danger, I think he'd do it. Send Alec in and Olson would be afraid to turn him down. It's men like Alec who elect him."

"Where does it get us?" Tully demanded. "What good would a deputy have been today?"

"A deputy could have gone in the Mahaffey, stopped everybody's work and demanded an accounting of everybody's time. If he did it often enough, I think he could make plenty of trouble for Ben."

Tully considered this. There was a certain shrewdness in what Sarah suggested. If he removed himself, the foreigner, from the picture Olson would be forced to intervene in a quarrel between the two local factions. It was a weapon of retaliation at most, and a kind of protection at the least. He would send Alec in. Sarah rose now, looking at her watch. "I've got a doctor's appointment now, Tully. What do you plan to do?"

"I've got to phone Denver for parts, then I'll pick up some lunch and take the tank out."

Sarah, walking over to her coat, said over her shoulder, "Snap the lock when you leave."

Tully said he would.

Sarah had almost reached the door when she halted, turned and said, "I'll buy you lunch at Joe's."

"Fine," Tully said, trying not to show the surprise he felt at her invitation.

Why did I say that? Sarah wondered as she descended the stone steps of the courthouse. All her stern resolutions to see little of Tully and to make that little as impersonal as possible had gone overboard already. She had promised herself that she would be firmly suspicious of him and mistrust his every move. Yet this morning she had sympathized with his troubles and had even arranged to have lunch with him. He was, she decided almost bitterly, getting to be a bad habit with her, one that was increasingly hard to break. *That's because of Kevin,* she thought, and she knew immediately that this wasn't true.

Turning into the Main Street, she noticed that the sky was beginning to haze over. There was some weather coming, she knew, and she wondered, almost fretfully, what a sleet or snow storm would do to the Sarah Moffit operations. It seemed that lately she did nothing but worry about the Sarah Moffit—or about Tully Gibbs.

Dr. Richards's ground-floor office next to the hardware store smelled of medicine and newly laid linoleum and its waiting room was empty of patients. The door in the far wall was open and when Sarah closed the street door Dr. Richards called, "Come on through, Sarah."

She crossed the waiting room and entered the consultation room. Dr. Richards, in shirt sleeves, was at the sink scrubbing syringes and placing them in the sterilizer nearby. He was a small man in his middle forties, certainly too thin, almost frail. His face seldom wore anything but the humorless, almost fretful expression that was on it now as he glanced over his shoulder.

Sarah, who loathed all pomposities, did not really like Dr. Richards, but she forgave him much because of his devotion to his profession. She said, "Hi, Doc," knowing it would irritate him, and slipped out of her coat which she dropped on the white metal chair. "Where is Mrs. Bjornsen?"

Dr. Richards frowned and said, "I can call her. Are you afraid to be alone with me long enough to get your cold shot?"

Sarah laughed. "I was teasing."

Dr. Richards only grunted and dried his hands. Since he was County Medical Officer, he and Sarah saw much of each other at the courthouse. When his duties occasionally brought him before the commissioners, Sarah always took his side against them, defending him almost to the point of insubordination. For the three commissioners with their rough country humor loved to bait him, to deride his skill as if he were a not-very-good veterinarian, and refused his most reasonable request for hours before giving in.

Sarah rolled up her sleeve as she watched Dr. Richards's

small, precise hands prepare the syringe and fill it with cold vaccine. This white-painted room with its cold metal cabinets, examining table and scales all painted white, too, seemed a fitting background for this bloodless little man, she thought.

Dr. Richards asked abruptly, "Did the commissioners kick about my last month's bills?"

"They never really do. They just like to tease you," Sarah said easily.

Dr. Richards came over with a wet swatch of alcohol-soaked cotton and scrubbed the spot beneath her shoulder joint. "I don't find them amusing," he observed stiffly.

"Well, you always have the last laugh, don't you?"

"How's that?"

"They're all your patients, aren't they? A blunt hypodermic needle, for instance, can make up for a lot of rude remarks."

Dr. Richards smiled sourly. "They're never sick. If I depended on them for a living, I'd starve."

Sarah remembered then, and she giggled.

"What's funny?"

"What about Justin Byers's gas?"

Dr. Richards's hands, poised for the shot, halted, and he looked blankly at Sarah. "His what?" he echoed.

"I said, what about Justin Byers's gas?"

"I don't know what you're talking about. He's never come to me for anything. Now, hold still, will you?"

He administered the shot expertly and when he was finished, Sarah continued. "He came to you about eleven o'clock last Monday, didn't he?"

"Certainly not. I was in Galena a week ago today."

He turned away to clean the syringe, and Sarah rose and reached for her coat. In her mind she was reviewing the exact happenings of last Monday morning. She was certain that after Tully left the commissioners' room Byers went out. He returned later, presumably after making a phone call. It was then he had announced that he would countersign the warrants later since he had an appointment with the doc.

"Come back a week from today," Dr. Richards said.

"All right," Sarah said. And then added, "Are you sure Byers didn't come to you Monday?"

Dr. Richards looked sharply and unpleasantly at her. "I haven't so many patients, Sarah, that I forget them. I've never treated Justin Byers for anything. I never see him except at commissioners' meetings."

Sarah shrugged. "It wasn't important. Goodbye."

Out on the street Sarah looked at her watch. It lacked a few minutes of noon, and she turned upstreet, leisurely heading for Joe's Restaurant. Dr. Richards's words about Byers, however, bothered her. She stubbornly remembered Byers's statement that he had a doctor's appointment. Since Dr. Richards was the only doctor in Azurite and since there was no dentist closer than Galena, his meaning was unmistakable. Carefully now she thought back. When Byers left the room he had turned left. Only the Assessor's office lay in that direction. If Byers had made a phone call it must have been made on the phone in that office.

Sarah was passing the hotel now and impulsively she slowed her pace, then turned and went into the lobby, heading for the phone booth. Once there, she called Ann Hoffman at the Assessor's office. After identifying herself, she said, "Ann, were you in the office last Monday morning?"

"All morning," Ann said. "Why?"

"Did Justin Byers come in the office around eleven o'clock? Remember, that was the day the commissioners met."

There was a short silence at the other end of the wire, and then abruptly Ann said, "Why, sure. He came in and asked to use the phone."

"You didn't hear any of the conversation, did you?"

Anne's voice took on a note of huffiness. "He made very sure I didn't. He sent me out of the room before he even started to dial. Why?"

"Nothing. Just county business. He promised to make a call and I never found out if he did or not. Thanks, Ann."

Sarah hung up and sat motionless in the booth. All she knew now was that Byers had made a phone call and lied publicly about the person he had called. He had also made the call seem urgent enough to leave the commissioners' meeting. Swiftly then, she reviewed what had taken place at the commissioners' meeting. There was nothing of importance that had occurred except the stubborn interview with Tully in which the commissioners rejected all Tully's requests for county aid. Turning that over in her mind, Sarah felt a growing curiosity. That interview with Tully must have been so important to Byers that he found it necessary to make an immediate call and to lie about it.

Slowly, Sarah rose and walked out into the lobby, heading for the street. She decided now that she was being a plain snoop. Yet the thought persisted, *Why should Byers lie?* There was something else about Byers, too, that Sarah wondered about now. During the past week Byers had been spending quite a bit of time in her office, looking at the county records. As a commissioner he had every right to do so, but it did seem a little strange. Added to this business of the phony call to the doctor it was all very mystifying. Probably the best thing to do was forget it, she thought, as she headed up the street toward the restaurant.

"I'd take you to dinner tonight," Sam said to Beth in the late afternoon, "except there isn't a joint in town where the food wouldn't poison a coyote. We can get a couple of cans of dog food and cook 'em over a hot plate if you want."

Beth was seated at her desk, and she looked over at Sam who was seated at his. "I've got a better idea than that. Come to our place for dinner."

Sam grimaced. "I want your company, not Mrs. Kelly's, thanks."

"I meant Ben's and my house."

Sam scowled. "And get a tomahawk buried in my skull?"

"Ben's out of town and will be for a week or so. It's perfectly safe."

At seven o'clock that evening Sam rang the doorbell of the Hodeses' house, and was admitted by Beth. She was wearing a gray gabardine dress and a red scarf at her throat, and as she stepped back, holding the door open, Sam whistled appreciatively even before he greeted her.

"Don't ever show up at the office looking like that," Sam said as he stepped in. "If you do you'll be fighting off all the wolves in town."

Beth blushed faintly, but Sam knew she was pleased. She took Sam's hat and coat and the package he offered, and then led the way into the living room, Sam following. The first time he had been in this room he had entered almost with fear and trembling, which turned out to be justified. He had quarreled with Ben Hodes and left in anger, and his memory of the place was unpleasant. Tonight, with Ben gone, the atmosphere was different, and he looked about him with pleasure. That the Hodeses were well off he already knew. Beth's father had owned and operated one of the most prosperous mines in Azurite. This room, the whole big house, reflected that wealth. The furniture was simply good and expensive, more masculine than feminine. Logs were crackling in the big fireplace, and Sam had the momentary impression of walking into the club of a very rich man.

Beth put the gin and vermouth on the small bar against the far wall, saying, "There's ice and a shaker here, boss."

Rubbing his hands together Sam came over to join her. He noted the olives, the pearl onions and the lemon rinds on the tray, and he said, "Looks like you've made these before."

Beth nodded. "Once," she said soberly, and both she and Sam laughed.

When Sam had finished making the pitcher of martinis and had poured their drinks, he raised his glass in a toast. "Happy Hooligan."

Beth said after tasting her drink, "That's one I never heard before."

"Oh, I'm full of surprises."

Beth looked directly at him. "You know you really are."

"Am I? Like what?"

Beth shrugged. "Well, like giving Ed the day off to go hunting, like being able to run a linotype yourself, like hiring me."

"You know," Sam said soberly and with total irrelevance, "you can really spell."

Beth threw back her head and laughed. "You make that sound as if it were in the same category with being able to dance well or to cook well."

Sam grinned. "It is."

Beth rose. "Speaking of cooking, I'd better take a look at our dinner. Come on out in the kitchen."

Sam lifted the pitcher of martinis on the tray and followed Beth through the hall and the dining room out into the immaculate kitchen. Seating himself at the table, he looked about him and decided that every known gadget relating to housekeeping was housed in this bright room. Beth stirred something on the stove, took a peek in the oven, switched on the ventilating fan, then produced from the oven a plate of warm thin toast covered with a linen napkin. Afterwards she took from a shelf the stand for a small chafing dish, lighted its alcohol lamp and from the oven drew out the chafing dish. Sam watched her curiously as she sat the dish on the stand then lifted the lid. "Good Lord, what's this?" Sam said.

"I'm a patsy for shad roe," Beth said seriously, as she lifted the lid off the dish.

Sam looked at the beautiful golden stuff and his mouth began to water. "You've got a whole week's wages tied up in that pot, lady."

Beth giggled. "It's only money." She scooped some of the shad roe onto one piece of toast and handed it to Sam. It melted deliciously in his mouth, and afterwards he sandwiched in a sip of martini and had another. Presently he leaned back in his chair, regarding Beth, and murmured, "I wonder what the peasants are doing."

"Eating cake."

"I can understand Ben's raising hell when you left," Sam said. "My God, it's a wonder he doesn't weigh three hundred pounds."

"He doesn't appreciate food," Beth said. "For him it's just something to kill hunger."

Sam poured out another martini for them, then said, "Speaking of that jolly character, did you hear that Tully's camp was shot up this morning?"

"Yes, I heard." Beth's glance held his. "Are you linking Ben with that?"

"Shouldn't I?"

"You think he'd shoot at a man?"

Sam held her gaze. "Yes."

Color came into Beth's face. "Ben was out of town."

"I know he was, but you asked me a question and I answered it."

"Ben's not that bad," Beth protested gently.

"He's a purple louse and you know it, Beth. Don't even try to defend him. It's as hopeless as trying to stuff warm butter down the throat of a wild jackass. He's a bully, he's got a tycoon complex and he's not bright. That's what I think of him in a few well-chosen words. Now, let's change the subject."

"Not quite yet," Beth said. She offered Sam some more shad roe and helped herself. "You mind me asking questions I shouldn't?"

"I won't even try to stop you."

"If you think Ben is behind all of Tully's trouble, you're wrong."

"Not necessarily Ben, but someone Ben's paying."

"You're wrong there, too."

Sam said dryly, "Look now, no violins, please. Just tell me where I'm wrong."

"Ben made it possible for Tully to open that mine."

"What?"

"But it's true," Beth insisted. "He loaned Tully ten thousand dollars."

Sam looked at her incredulously, then snorted. "You better lay off the tea, kid."

"It's true, Sam. I got in on the tail end of it and that was only by accident. Remember when Tully gave Ben a thrashing at the Elks party?"

Sam nodded.

"Next day Tully came here to talk with Ben. I only overheard the last part of their conversation. I think they had a bet on the outcome of the fight. It was a ten-thousand-dollar bet."

Sam whistled in surprise. "Where would Tully get any ten thousand to put up?"

"I don't think it was that kind of bet," Beth said. "If Tully won, Ben was to loan him ten thousand, no collateral. If Tully lost, he was to stay away from Sarah."

Sam slowly sipped his martini, pondering this information. This accounted for Tully's capital. Moreover, if Tully had bet Ben the night of the fight at the Elks Club, that was *before* Kevin had offered him a half share of the Sarah Moffit. *Fantastic,* Sam thought, and the rebel in him felt a small delight. Tully not only had the nerve to forge letters from Jimmy Russel, but he also had the gall to suggest and collect on this lunatic bet before he even knew that Kevin would have any part of him. *A real parlay,* Sam mused. *There's an operator.*

He was called back to the present by Beth's voice. "Does that make Ben out a dog?"

"You mean just because he didn't welsh on his bet?"

Beth nodded, and Sam was silent a moment, thinking about this. Yes, it all fitted together, he thought, now that he had all the facts. Ben's actions and Tully's worries made great good sense. He looked at Beth and smiled crookedly. "How long was the note for?"

"I looked in the bank files—I'm a director, you know. The note was for one hundred twenty days."

Sam lifted the pitcher of martinis and refilled Beth's glass, then he said, "Lady, you don't know what you've just said." He paused. "Do you?"

"Certainly I do."

"If you do, then add it up, it'll come out like this. If Ben can keep Tully from getting out enough ore in one hundred and twenty days to pay back that loan, he'll move in on Tully like a Sherman tank. Tully's only assets are his share in the Sarah Moffit. Ben'll get them. Simple, isn't it?"

For still seconds Beth looked at Sam, and Sam realized, almost with shame, that Beth had never before really believed in Ben's guilt, and that now suddenly she did. He felt an overwhelming pity for her in this moment, but he held his silence. *It's part of growing up,* he thought.

Beth finished her drink, then rose and said brightly, "You have another drink and I'll get dinner on."

They chatted on inconsequential things during dinner, and Sam found himself enormously eager to learn more about Beth. From just a pretty but spineless girl she had turned for him into a generous and courageous person who was starved for affection. It would be pleasant to give her that affection, Sam was beginning to think.

After dinner she and Sam did the dishes and then retired to the living room. There had been no further mention of Ben, and Sam wondered if Beth had forgiven him for his brutal directness in discussing her brother.

Beth poured brandy into two big snifters and handed one to Sam, then sat down beside him on the sofa. For a moment they idly watched the fire, then Beth said soberly, "I hope Tully makes it, Sam."

"All right-thinking citizens do," Sam said.

"Is he a nice guy really?" Beth asked.

Sam wondered how he should answer this. Should he say "Sure, he's just hungry," or "Not quite," or "No, he's a stinker?" Surprisingly, he found himself saying, "Yes, really nice."

Oddly, the question seemed important to Beth. Also she seemed completely satisfied by Sam's answer, and he was to remember this later.

Beth rose now and put some Mozart on the record player by the bar, then she and Sam talked shop for an hour in an easy, friendly way. Sam discovered himself telling her his most private hopes and ambitions.

When he remembered to look at his watch, he rose. "Good Lord. I'm windier than a Georgia congressman. It's late."

Beth rose, almost reluctantly, offered him a drink for the road which he declined, and then she came with him to the door.

His hand on the knob, Sam turned to look down at Beth. "You know," he said soberly, "I made a threat once I never carried out."

Surprisingly, Beth said, "I know you did."

Sam kissed her then, found it very good, kissed her again, then stepped outside, saying good night and thanks over his shoulder. He had not even reached the street walk before he said to himself *You slob, you're in love and you know it.*

That evening as Sarah was about to close the office, old Judge Apperson strolled in. He was an aging, small, dirty, irascible old man who had once prospered as an expert on mining law in Azurite's boom days. In later years he had fallen on hard times and was now a sort of chore boy for anyone with a grudge who was willing to take it to court.

He laid a document on the counter and said abruptly, "How's Harve?"

"A little better, according to Emma," Sarah said.

"How long since he's been down?"

"Oh, weeks."

"Well, tell him I asked about him," the judge grunted. He tapped the document. "I want to record this."

Sarah took the paper and moved over to the register. It was a warranty deed on a mining claim, Sarah saw. She opened the registry and began to record it. At first the name of the claim, Jote Smith, meant nothing to her, but when she noted that the property was being conveyed to the Mahaffey she frowned.

Looking up at Judge Apperson she said, "Where's the Jote Smith? I've forgotten."

"It's one of those claims old man Carpenter has been nursing in his bosom for twenty-five years."

"Toward Vicksburg Hill?" Sarah asked.

"I reckon."

Sarah finished the recording, appending the recording date and book number on the deed. As she handed the deed back to Judge Apperson, she said, "If that's the claim I'm thinking of, there's an easement on it."

The judge looked sternly at her. "Well, young lady, an easement is conveyed with the property. What of it?"

"Nothing," Sarah said. "That'll be a quarter, Judge."

Judge Apperson paid up, said goodbye and left. For a moment Sarah stared at the door the Judge had closed behind him. It was curious that the Mahaffey should be showing interest in this claim now. Old man Carpenter had been trying to sell his claims at bargain prices for the last ten years, with no takers. Sarah wondered if Ben, who was a good geologist, had discovered that the Jote Smith straddled the same formation as the Vicksburg Claims, and was thereby hoping to profit if the Sarah Moffit profited. She remembered, too, that the road to the Sarah Moffit crossed the Jote Smith.

There was no use speculating, however, on Ben Hodes's intentions. He must recognize the easement, and that was all that really concerned her, she thought, as she turned toward the vault to lock up for the day.

There was a raw wind blowing as she stepped outside. The sky was overcast and as she hurried home past the lighted stores, she looked forward to a comfortable evening at home alone. She could wash her hair, do her nails and listen to music. Tully surely would have found a new cook and left for the mine by now.

Climbing the stairs to her apartment, she recalled her lunch with Tully today. He had been restless, still angry, impatient and oddly very gentle, and she found herself almost forgetting that he must be watched unceasingly. Ben's badgering of them would continue, she knew, but deep within her she felt it would always stop short of real trouble.

Ben's pride had been hurt and his plans crossed up, but he was too cunning to jeopardize his career by a really reckless mistake.

Mrs. Moffit was reading the paper as Sarah let herself into the warm and cozy apartment. "Hi, Ma! What's for dinner?" she asked as she hung up her coat.

"You have to ask? Can't you smell it?"

Sarah sniffed. "Shrimp?"

"Curried shrimp."

"That's good. Want a drink?"

"Just a little one."

Sarah went out to the kitchen and mixed a couple of weak highballs, came back to the living room, handed one to her mother, sank into a chair and kicked her shoes off. She could hear the wind tugging at the window, and as she sipped contentedly on her drink she heard the first spatter of rain. It would later turn into sleet, she supposed, and she wondered if all the hunters camped in wretched flapping tents and nursing their precious fires didn't wish they were home tonight. She knew they didn't, but thought they should.

Idly, contentedly, she watched her mother finish reading the paper while sipping at her drink. Carefully, Mrs. Moffit folded the paper and said, "Anything exciting happen today, dear?"

"Nothing with me, but plenty with Tully." She told Mrs. Moffitt of the shooting at the mine and of Tully's visit to the sheriff. Mrs. Moffit smiled faintly at mention of Sheriff Olson.

"But that's absurd," she said when Sarah finished. "Ben's out of town. He couldn't have done it."

"Ma, you're being simple again," Sarah said patiently. "Ben is paying someone to do it. Probably one of his miners or mill hands." She frowned. "Why are you sticking up for Ben? You loathe him and you always have. Admit it."

"Well, I've never really liked him," Mrs. Moffit conceded. "Still, it just doesn't seem sensible. Why should he want to stop Kevin and Tully from opening a mine? He's got a mine of his own and a very good one. He doesn't need money. Why should he risk it all by making all this trouble?"

"It might be partly me, Ma."

Mrs. Moffit looked sharply at her. "You mean he's jealous of Tully?"

"Could be."

"Are you giving him any grounds for jealousy?"

"No," Sarah said slowly. "It wouldn't take much of a shove though."

"Then why don't you?" Mrs. Moffit said matter-of-factly.

Sarah rose, and in her stocking feet went over and turned on the radio. As it was warming up she glanced over at her mother. "You like him?"

"Of course I do."

"What if he turned out to be a crook?"

"I'd still like him. Why? Is he?"

"I wish I knew, Ma," Sarah said. "I wish I did."

"Feel like telling me about it?"

"I honestly don't," Sarah said. Then the radio cut in and the moment was lost. Sarah listened to the news, then went out to help her mother with dinner. They ate in the warm kitchen, listening to the rain pelt softly at the window.

Mrs. Moffit reminded Sarah that tonight the Library Board met, and that she dreaded it. The Board consisted of three ladies whom the town considered genteel. That they were, Mrs. Moffit conceded, but they also knew nothing of books, and at times seemed to hate the printed word. They were incessantly demanding censorship of the new library acquisitions, and it took a fine sense of tact for Mrs. Moffit to gently stand them off and still retain her job. She would do it again tonight, Sarah knew.

Dinner finished, Mrs. Moffit took off for the Board meeting. Sarah cleaned up, put on a stack of records, then washed her hair, leaving the bathroom door open so she could listen.

Afterwards, while her hair dried, she sat in the living room and did her nails.

An hour passed thus. Combing out her pale, curling hair,

she was trying to make up her mind if she really liked the Bartok piece when a heavy knock came at the door. It was imperious and somehow so demanding that Sarah rose quickly and with the towel still about her shoulders answered the door.

It was Tully. Sarah's heart seemed to do a small nip-up at the sight of him. Drops of rain clung to his flushed face, and his slicker had already shed pools of water on the corridor floor. "I got some news," he announced grimly. "Can I come in?"

Sarah said, "Of course. What is it, Tully?"

He tramped into the room and then halted as Sarah shut the door.

"Picked up my cook around dark and headed for the mine," Tully began. "You know where the road curves around that gully?"

"No."

"Well, anyway, somebody brought a chain saw up there and laid fifteen big spruce trees down across the road."

"How childish!" Sarah said angrily. "This is really fantastic, Tully."

"Oh, brother, you don't know how fantastic. Nailed to the first downed tree was a nice neat sign. It said, 'Road closed by order of the owner.'"

That's it, Sarah thought suddenly. That's the Jote Smith Claim. For full seconds Sarah considered this. This was the claim whose conveyance Judge Apperson had recorded only this afternoon. Had Ben bought the claim, hoping that the easement would not be conveyed also? Sarah doubted it, since his attorney acknowledged the fact.

Swiftly then Sarah described Judge Apperson's recording of the deed this afternoon, and what she supposed lay behind it.

"But Kevin's got easements through all those claims our road crosses, hasn't he?" Tully asked.

"Of course he has."

"Then let's get them," Tully said flatly. "I'll have the

sheriff and my own chain saw out there by eight o'clock in the morning." He started for the door.

"Wait, Tully, I'll go with you."

Remembering the open jeep, Sarah got her raincoat, galoshes and ski cap from the closet, and then tramped down into the rainy night beside Tully.

As Tully turned into the river bottom, they could see Kevin's lights were still on. Halting the jeep in front of the house, Tully handed Sarah out.

Their knock on the door was answered by Kevin who still held in his hand the newspaper he had been reading when he was interrupted.

"Come in, come in," old Kevin said. "What are you two youngsters doing out on a night like this?"

"An emergency, Mr. Russel," Tully said.

Old Kevin led the way back to the kitchen which was warm and tight against the night. Once their raincoats were removed and they were seated at the table, Tully told of the roadblock. Old Kevin listened carefully. As Tully finished with his account he asked, "You have an easement on that Jote Smith Claim, haven't you, Mr. Russel?"

Old Kevin nodded. "From Bill Carpenter, yes. I'll get it."

Sarah heard Tully breathe an audible sigh of relief. Slowly old Kevin moved toward the living-room desk, rummaged around and presently returned with a sheaf of documents held by a rubber band. He seated himself, almost with ceremony, and removed the rubber band, then sorted through the documents. He came up with one he handed to Tully, saying gently, "There it is, boy."

Tully opened the form and saw that the easement was properly signed by Carpenter.

Sarah said, "May I see it?" Tully extended it and she took one look at the easement. Then a feeling that was almost physical sickness came to her, and the paper slipped from her hand.

"What's the matter?" Tully demanded.

Sarah raised her glance to Tully's face and she felt an overwhelming misery. "It's not recorded, Tully. It's worthless. Ben can close the road." She shifted her glance to old Kevin who was staring at her with an unbelieving expression.

"But Carpenter signed them," old Kevin said.

Sarah only shook her head as Tully skirted the table and picked up the document to look at it again.

"No, Kevin," Sarah said bitterly. "Carpenter probably sold Ben the claim believing your easement would be honored, but since your easement wasn't recorded it just doesn't exist for the new owner."

Now she looked up at Tully and saw the shock in his eyes. "You mean our only road to the mine is blocked?" Tully asked.

Sarah nodded. "How could I do that, Tully? Don't you see, I'm the one to blame! I work at the Clerk's Office. I record these every day—and I didn't think to remind Kevin to record them." The tears were here now and uncontrollable, and even Tully's rough jacket to cry on didn't help.

7

It was sleeting the next morning when Tully, just after daylight, rode horseback out of town leading a pack horse with the compressor tank lashed to its back. He was making sure, at the price of his own discomfort, that the tank would be delivered today. To skirt the roadblock and the old Jote Smith Claim in the jeep would have meant bushwhacking in the deep gully among tangled timber and ground already soaked by a night's rain. Horses were surer.

He arrived at the camp soaked to the skin a little after noon. In the warm cook tent, while he had a sandwich and downed several cups of coffee, he told Alec of Kevin's forgetting to record the easements. In a backwoods country, especially among elderly people who had been their own lawyers for a half century, it was a common occurrence that property owners neglected to record deeds and conveyances. Tully didn't have to explain this to Alec. And Alec, tired, wet too, a deepening gloom settling upon his hard stubbled face, heard him out in silence. The news was so staggering that Alec did not even seem angry.

"So what do we do?" Alec asked.

Tully tiredly scrubbed his cheek with his open palm.

"Keep pitching. We've got grub for a month, and the new cook will be out this afternoon. When the parts come for the cat, I'll pack them in. Get the ore above ground. Right now the road will have to wait."

"What road? How you going to jump the Jote Smith Claim—build an overhead highway?"

"I don't know," Tully said. "There must be a way."

"What way?" Alec insisted. "It's forest land on either side of you. Those Forest Service characters won't let you touch it. Even if they made a special consideration, it would take six months for you to clear through Washington. This is Wilderness Area, boy. Strictly holy."

Tully put down his cup. "I know."

Alec had summed it up neatly. There was no road possible that did not cross the Jote Smith Claim. It might be possible, by delving into county records, to piece together enough adjoining claims in this national forest to reach the Sarah Moffit. Yet, any substitute road built on these claims would be fantastically impractical, and would cost a fortune, even if it were possible to get the easements. The county naturally would refuse to condemn a right-of-way through the Jote Smith Claim. In short, he could mine ore, build new bins and fill them, and still the ore would remain on the Vicksburg Claims.

"I'll be getting along," he said, and he began to button up his slicker.

Alec watched him morosely. "What do I tell the boys?"

"Just what I've told you," Tully said. "They get paid. The transport problem is my own."

The ride back to town was almost as dismal and cold as the ride out. The sleet sometime during the afternoon turned into snow. Low clouds on the peaks and the whole dripping forest seemed to be bracing itself for winter.

Hunched in his saddle, Tully again tried to see a way out of their dilemma, but thinking of it he could only remember Sarah's misery of last night. Her failure to record Kevin's easements was the first sign of imperfection he had seen in her, and somehow it made her more dear to him. They had left old Kevin stunned and half sick at his own carelessness. Sarah's state of mind had been little better. She bitterly blamed herself for having overlooked something so obvious she had never even thought of it. In the apartment later, after leaving Kevin, while she made a pot of coffee, Tully had watched her, and a growing concern for her came to him. This, after all, did not really touch her materially. The Sarah Moffit Mine could peacefully die and nothing in her life would be changed, nor would anything in Kevin's life. But Sarah had seemed crushed and, what was worse, shamed to the depths of her being. When Tully had said good night and kissed her, she had clung to him almost with desperation. It was as if their common disaster had brought a new and tender intimacy to them.

By dark it was really snowing and it was beginning to freeze, making the footing treacherous for the horses. Added to that, Tully felt the old trouble coming; his legs had turned totally numb. Wretchedly, he hung on to the saddle horn, wondering if his feet would freeze while he was unable to feel any sensation at all in his legs. An hour of the purest misery followed, but at last feeling began to return to his legs.

When he reached town and dismounted at the stable where he had rented the horses, he clung to the saddle horn, laboriously exercising his legs until full feeling returned. Afterwards, he tramped back to the hotel in the mounting slush and ice of the street, and he was truly cold. Asking for his key from the clerk, he was so stupid weary that he did not notice the note that the clerk deposited on the counter along with the key.

Turning towards the stairs, he heard the clerk say, "Don't you want this?"

Tully turned, shaking with the cold, and stared blankly at the clerk, and only a second later saw the note. He retrieved it and read it haltingly. It was from Sarah, asking him to come over to the *Nugget* office when he got in.

Once in dry clothes, Tully went downstreet to the restaurant and ate a quick order of ham and eggs, and then tramped back to the *Nugget* office. The lights within cast an orange glow on the gray slush that scummed the sidewalk, and the thin snow held on.

Through the glass of the door, Tully could see that Sarah,

Sam and Beth were waiting behind the counter inside. At his entrance, Sam lifted a hand in grim salutation. Beth said hello and Tully answered, looking immediately, carefully, at Sarah. Perhaps it was the bright color of her plaid dress that made her face seem pale by contrast. In spite of the smile she gave Tully, she looked tired and depressed, and Tully wondered if his own face reflected the same low spirits.

"We've saved a box seat at the wailing wall," Sam said, indicating the chair beside Beth. Sarah sat on Beth's desk, her long legs crossed. There was an open bottle of whiskey on Sam's desk, and he held the glass cradled in his hand.

Tully swung the chair around, straddled it, folded his arms on its back while Sam drank off the rest of his drink, then extended his glass and the bottle to Tully. "We got one glass, so this is the loving cup," he growled.

"No, thanks." Tully declined, as did Sarah.

When Sam offered the bottle to Beth, she declined, too. Then Sam looked at her disapprovingly. "Okay, get sulky," he murmured. He poured out a half glass of whiskey, then rose, skirted the counter and went back into the composing room to the water tap.

Tully glanced up at Sarah and surprised her watching him, an open concern in her face. "Bad trip?" she asked.

"A wet one." Tully shifted his weight in the chair. "Has anything else come unstuck since I left?"

Beth murmured, "What else could?"

Sam returned then and sank heavily into the chair. "The first thing I did this morning was check on the Land Records," Sarah said. "Ben was right. The easements weren't recorded." The old look of guilt and shame fleetingly crossed her face. Sam's eyes were oddly gentle, and he said nothing. But Tully, watching Sarah, saw her expression alter almost imperceptibly, as if once she acknowledged her shame a tough and stubborn pride still remained.

Sarah lit a cigarette, and then said, "Besides eating worms all day I've been doing something else. Anyone interested in hearing what about?"

"If it's a post-mortem, no," Sam said gently. "Quit beating yourself over the head, will you, Sarah?"

"Not quite yet," Sarah replied. "The thing that's bothered me all day is how Ben knew those easements weren't recorded."

"The Land Records are a public record, aren't they?" Sam said. "Anybody can look at them."

"That's just it. Nobody has while I wasn't around—except one man."

"Who was that?" Tully asked.

"Justin Byers."

Sarah nodded when Tully cut in. "Would Byers have had a chance to check on the Land Records?"

"He's the only one who did have," Sarah said flatly. "Oh, other people have asked to check something, but they've always asked me to do it for them."

There was a long silence then, while each of them tried to read some significance into this.

Sam at last said shrewdly, "Keep talking, Sarah."

Sarah hesitated. "All right, I will," she said then. "Maybe what I'm going to say adds up to zero. Maybe not. But I got to thinking today that Byers's visits started only after the last commissioners' meeting."

"The one where they bounced me around?" Tully asked.

Sarah nodded. "Remember what happened at that meeting, Tully?"

"I'll never forget it."

"All right, let me tell you what happened after you left." She described then how Byers had left the room and returned in a few minutes presumably after making a phone call, for he had stated that he had a doctor's appointment, and must leave.

"I didn't pay any attention to it at the time," Sarah continued. "But yesterday I had an appointment with Dr. Richards." She went on to tell of the conversation that took place in the doctor's office, relating how she had teased Dr. Richards about the treatment he received from the commissioners. She told of her suggestion that Dr. Richards could get even with the commissioners when they came to him as patients.

"You know what he said then?" Sarah asked. "He said he'd never treated a commissioner. Remembering that Byers said that morning he had an appointment with the doc, I asked him especially if he wasn't treating Justin Byers. He said he'd never seen him in a professional way."

Sarah paused, looking briefly at each of them. "That got me curious," Sarah went on. "When I left Dr. Richards's I got to wondering why Byers should lie about a doctor's appointment. Then I got an idea. I was passing the hotel, so I went in to the phone booth and called Ann Hoffman."

"The gal in the Assessor's Office?" Sam asked.

"Yes. Remember when Byers left the commissioners he turned left toward her office. Well, I called Ann and asked if Byers had made a phone call in her office the morning of the commissioners' meeting. When she said he had, I asked her if she knew who he called. She said he was very careful to make sure she didn't know." Sarah paused as if to emphasize this. "Byers sent her out of the room."

Sam whistled softly. "Back up a minute, Sarah. What went on at that commissioners' meeting that would make Byers put in a quick call afterwards, then lie about having to leave?"

"That's just it," Sarah said. "Nothing went on except Tully's asking for help."

"A farmer wanted a culvert removed, remember?" Tully put in.

"That's right," Sarah agreed. "Those two things."

Tully looked searchingly at Sam.

Sam said slowly, summing it up, "You think Byers had a chance to see the Land Records. You think he got curious only after the commissioners' meeting. You think he made a call and lied about it."

Sarah only nodded.

Beth put in, "Considering that Ben bought the Jote Smith Claim, what more proof do you need that Byers told Ben?"

"You're only guessing, Beth. We have no proof," Sam said.

Tully remembered his call at the Mahaffey yesterday morning, and an idea came to him.

"Beth, hasn't your brother a couple of old battle axes working for him out there?"

Beth smiled. "That's right. My father hired them."

Tully looked at his watch. "You suppose they stay up as late as eight-thirty?"

"Not much later."

Tully looked then at Sarah. "Sarah, you know them?"

"I know Olive Lindsay better than I know Hilda Pruitt. Why?"

"Get set to put over a snow-job then," Tully said grimly. "Call her right now. Tell her you've been meaning to call her for the last week and just remembered it tonight. Tell her Justin Byers lost a license plate from his car about a week or ten days ago. Ask her if they found it at the Mahaffey. When she says no, ask her if he wasn't out there the Monday morning of the commissioners' meeting."

Sam's soft chuckle broke in as Tully finished, and Tully looked at him. There was an appreciation in Sam's eyes, Tully saw, but beyond it there was a shrewdness, a look of total understanding that made Tully suddenly uncomfortable. "You're a real cutie," Sam said gently. "You're wily, my friend. You have a great future."

Tully could not tell what lay behind Sam's gentle mockery. For the moment it was disturbing. He looked at Sarah and said, "Want to call?"

Without further hesitation, Sarah reached for the phone. Everyone in the room heard Olive Lindsay's irritable voice as she answered the phone.

"Were you in bed, Olive? Good. You'll think I'm crazy," Sarah said, "but I just remembered something that I should have remembered a week ago." Then she followed Tully's instructions and asked after the missing license plate.

Olive's snappy answer was negative.

"But Justin was out there, wasn't he? It was on a Monday. The Monday of the commissioners' meeting." There was a long silence, and Tully found himself straining to catch the expression on Sarah's face. The receiver vibrated shrilly, and then Sarah said, "Thank you, Olive," and hung up. She looked directly at Tully. "Yes, that's where he went."

Tully found himself holding his breath, and he exhaled softly.

"So Byers is our boy," Sam murmured. "He calls Ben as soon as he finds out what Tully is up to, then he goes out to see him, then he snoops for a week in the County Clerk's Office. He comes up with Kevin's mistake, tells Ben, and Ben lowers the boom." Sam tilted back in his chair, clasped his hands behind his neck and looked thoughtfully at the ceiling. "I underestimated that kid brother of yours, Beth," he said finally. "I didn't figure he was in the business of buying commissioners."

Beth said nothing, only watched Sam.

Sam looked benignly at her. "You about to pull this family loyalty act again?"

Beth only shook her head. "No, I'm cured, Sam."

Sam looked at Tully. "You think Byers did it for love, Tully?"

"There's a way we can find out," Tully said slowly. He looked at Beth, now, and added, "Or rather there's a way Beth can."

Beth's eyes widened in surprise. In her expression was the hesitant yet prideful look of a person who knows a dare is coming. "How can I?"

"Who owns the bank?" Tully demanded.

"Why, Ben and I do."

"As co-owner you have every right to look at the books, haven't you?"

"I'm a director. Yes."

"Then tomorrow go in and tell Harry Bogue you want to look at the books. Tell him to take the day off and go fishing."

"Then what?" Beth asked.

"Then check on your brother's cash withdrawals. Check on Justin Byers's cash deposits. If they jibe within a few days, we'll have ammunition for a grand jury."

Beth said softly, "I'll just do that."

But Tully wasn't finished. He said, "You own stock in the Mahaffey, Beth?"

Beth laughed shortly. "About half of it."

"All right, then check on the Mahaffey stockholders. Especially check on recent transfers of stock." He paused. "Can stock be transferred without your consent?"

"It started out that way, but it didn't last long. I wanted to give the widow of one of our workmen some of my stock and Ben objected. So I objected when he wanted to transfer some. Now, we just go our own ways."

"Then check the recent transfers."

"I'll just do that too," Beth said, almost grimly.

Harry Bogue had scarcely opened the vault the next morning when Beth Hodes entered the bank. Instead of approaching one of the three windows, Beth went to the end of the wicket and came through the door that led into the working part of the bank.

Drawing off her gloves, she passed the bookkeeping girl at the calculator, spoke to the assistant cashier, also a woman, and stepped into Bogue's private office.

"Morning, Harry." There was something in the tone of Beth's voice that made Bogue faintly but instantly uneasy. In his constant dealings with the Hodeses, Bogue had long since written off Beth as someone deserving of politeness, but not much else. Yet her voice this morning was that of a woman of authority who was being civil, but only civil, to a paid employee.

Bogue rose belatedly, stood holding in his hand an insurance contract that he had been reading.

"I'm going to make a nuisance out of myself today, Harry. Give me a corner where I won't disturb you."

Bogue stared shrewdly at her from behind his rimless

glasses. "That's easy," he said finally. "You want into your safe-deposit box?"

Beth shook her head in negation, and said crisply, "I want to go over the balance sheets of our depositors."

It took five long seconds for Bogue to fully comprehend this strange request. Then he said curiously, "Anyone in particular?"

"Let's just start with the A's and work on through."

Bogue frowned, then cleared his throat nervously. He speculated for a moment on the reason for Beth's request, and he came up with nothing. Moreover, here was an outsider poaching on his own preserve. He looked sternly at Beth and said, "That's an unusual request," in a slow tentative voice. "You know that is highly confidential information."

"Come off it, Harry," Beth said. "As a stockholder and director of this bank, I can look at anything in here except the contents of safe-deposit box holders."

"True," Bogue murmured. He was suddenly embarrassed by Beth's bluntness. "Where would you like to work?"

"That's up to you."

The room was a small one, but in the rear toward the vault was a desk flanked by two chairs where Bogue took customers for the more confidential type of talk. Bogue cleared off the desk, seated Beth at it and then wheeled in the truck containing the first half-dozen balance-sheet ledgers.

Beth thanked him, and Bogue left her. Retreating to his office he closed the door, drew out a cigar, lighted it and then contemplated the calendar on the wall above his desk. Something was happening. Along with the rest of the town and county, he had heard about the quarrel between Beth and her brother. He had refused to discuss it in public, but in private with Mrs. Bogue he had speculated with deep interest on the cause of the quarrel and its effect upon him. He had agreed with his wife that he should take neither side —up to a point. When that point was reached, he must place himself definitely on the side of Ben.

He kept that firmly in mind during the next few minutes as he prowled past Beth's desk on made-up errands which took him into the vault. Beth was working on the B's when he first passed her. On his second cruise he noticed that the B ledger had been replaced and that the H ledger was missing.

Once in the vault he decided to risk it. Picking up the air-foam cushion from a chair that faced the cubbyhole shelf for the use of safe-deposit box owners, he left the vault and went straight to Beth's desk and halted. Beth looked up inquiringly.

"Beth, if you're going to work there you might as well be comfortable," Bogue said, and indicated a cushion. "Let me fix it for you."

"Oh, thank you," Beth said, rising.

Harry made a pretense of adjusting the cushion to the chair. Bent over so that his eyes were screened from Beth, he glanced quickly at the open ledger. In that split second before he straightened up, smiled and left, he saw that Beth had been studying Ben's balance sheet.

Back in his office, Bogue closed the door behind him, then opened it an inch and watched Beth. In a matter of minutes she rose and went over to the bookkeeper. In a moment the bookkeeper stood up, retreated to the vault and presently came out with several boxes of microfilm which she inserted in the Recordak. This was a machine which photographed each check on microfilm and then projected the microfilm on the small screen at the machine's base.

Bogue watched the bookkeeper insert the microfilm and then slowly turn the crank. Beth watched the screen for a couple of minutes, then dismissed the girl and handled the crank herself. Suddenly Bogue's phone rang.

The jangle startled him and he swore softly before closing the door to answer it. He spent the next fifteen minutes discussing details of an insurance policy with one of the local garage owners, and all that time he could barely control his patience. When the call was finished, he went over to the door again, opened it an inch and peered out. Beth was gone and the bookkeeper was back at her calculator.

Bogue moved over to the girl and halted beside her. When she looked up, Bogue said, "What did she want?"

"Miss Hodes? She was looking over the canceled checks."

"I know that," Bogue said irritably. "What was she after?"

"She didn't say. She asked for the last ten days' microfilm."

"You haven't any idea what she was after?"

"No sir, Mr. Bogue. All I know is while I was operating the machine she stopped the crank on several of Mr. Hodes's checks."

"What else did she want?"

"She looked at the deposit slips for the last ten days, then she left."

Bogue grunted and went back into his office. Gently he closed the door and sat down. As a member of the Board of Directors and as a forty-three per cent stockholder in the bank, Beth had every right to do what she was doing. Still Bogue knew that Ben, especially in view of his quarrel with Beth, would hotly resent her snooping. He knew that if Ben were here she would never have tried it.

By now the bank's doors were open and Bogue was in the thick of the day's business. But the memory of Beth's visit lay in the back of his mind, building up through the next hour into a nagging indefinable worry.

It took just one phone call to push him to his decision. Around eleven o'clock he received this call.

"Harry?"

Bogue instantly recognized the irritable, scolding voice of Olive Lindsay. "Yuh," Harry answered.

"Something's going on out here and I don't know what to do about it. Maybe you can help me."

"Yuh," Bogue said wearily.

"Beth's been out here wanting to see the company books. She's in Ben's office now with a list of stockholders. What do I do?"

Bogue sat up, alarm stilling him for a long moment.

"If you want to keep your job, you let her," Bogue said.

He could hear Olive snort. "She's up to no good, you can bet."

"That's not for you to judge," Bogue said stuffily.

Gently Bogue cradled the phone. For perhaps fifteen seconds he considered the information which Olive had passed on to him. Then he lifted the receiver, dialed the operator and when he had her, said, "Long Distance, get me the Brown Palace in Denver. I want to speak to Mr. Ben Hodes, person to person."

Both Sarah and Sam Horne were already in the restaurant when Tully stepped in the door. He looked inquiringly at Sarah even before saying good morning, and he saw immediately that they had had no word from Beth yet.

Sam growled, "I ought to be at work. Order me another cup of coffee, will you, Tully?"

Tully went over to the counter to leave the order, glancing at the clock on his way. It was after ten and Beth should have her information by now.

Carrying two cups of coffee back to the booth, Tully sat down. "You figure Bogue is giving her a hard time?" he asked.

"Not that guy," Sam said. "Not to anybody by the name of Hodes. I'll bet by now he's wrung his hands until they're bleeding." At that moment Tully heard the door open and glanced up. It was Beth. As she approached, Tully tried to read in her face the news she had for them, and he felt a sudden discouragement. There was no elation there, nothing but a kind of baffled concern.

Beth slipped into the seat beside Sam. He demanded brusquely, "What did you turn up?"

Beth drew off her gloves. "At the bank, nothing," she said in a discouraged voice. "Ben wrote one check for cash for five hundred dollars. I'm sure that was to pay for his convention trip. Byers had a couple of small deposits, but they were both by check."

Tully felt a leaden weight of discouragement settle within him. Beneath the table top, Sarah reached over and put her hand in his as if in silent sympathy.

"What about at the Mahaffey?" Sam asked.

"I got the list of stockholders and the list of recent stock transfers," Beth said, delving into her purse. "Frankly they don't mean anything to me."

"Any within the last ten days?" Tully asked.

Beth pulled the slip of paper from her purse and consulted her list. "Yes, one. It was ten shares to the Gold Medal Live Stock Association, whoever they are."

"What's the date of that transfer?" Tully asked.

"Last week."

Tully swiveled his glance to Sarah, then looked again at Beth. "What's the address of this Gold Medal Live Stock Association?"

Again Beth consulted her paper. "Galena."

Tully looked wonderingly at Sarah. "Ben in the cattle business?" Tully murmured. "Does that make sense, Beth?"

Beth shrugged. "News to me."

Sarah said softly then, "Wait a minute. Let me on the phone, Tully."

Tully rose and followed Sarah back to the phone booth in the rear. When he heard her ask for long distance and then for the County Clerk at the Galena County Courthouse, he dutifully held out a handful of change. When Sarah had made her deposit, she identified herself as the deputy County Clerk at Azurite. "I wonder if you could give me some information?" She went on, "Your county has a file of Trade Name Affidavits. I wonder if you'd look up the Gold Medal Live Stock Association affidavit. That's right, Gold Medal. I'd like to know whose signatures appear on it."

Sarah settled back against the wall, looking up at Tully.

"What's this?" Tully demanded.

"State law," Sarah said. "Anybody doing business under anything but his own name has to file a trade-name affidavit. It's—" Sarah straightened up and said into the phone— "yes?"

She listened intently, and then said in a quavering voice, "I've got it. Thank you very much."

Her hand holding the receiver sank to her lap as she looked up at Tully.

"The Gold Medal Live Stock Association affidavit was signed by Justin Byers and William Wishnack."

By noon Sarah had come to an important decision. She knew now that Tully had his weapon which he would use ferociously against Ben. Chances were that Ben was checked for good.

That left one more thing to clean up, Sarah decided—the matter of Tully's dishonesty. It was only fair to Kevin to tell him, and yet she shrank from seeing him. Today she had avoided him once. It had been Sam who carried the good news to old Kevin that morning while she had busied herself getting a ride for Tully on a truck going to Galena. And yet Kevin must be told and told soon, Sarah decided.

At twelve o'clock she locked up the office, her mind made up. But as she stepped out into the gray day and headed toward the apartment, her resolution began to waver. Once Tully was home with photostats of the Trade Name affidavit, it would be a time for festivity and celebration. It seemed cruel and heartless to wreck their good spirits by stripping Tully of all honor in front of Kevin.

A block ahead of her, she saw Beth leave the *Nugget* office and head upstreet, and she knew that Sam would be alone during the lunch hour. On impulse she turned into the *Nugget* office, stamping the slush from her overshoes before she entered. Sam, coatless, was seated at his typewriter, and when he heard the door close he looked up, grinned, rose and came over to the counter. "Tully get off?"

Sarah nodded. "What did Kevin say?"

"Say?" Sam echoed. "He couldn't say anything. He just stood there and grinned like a kid walking into the living room on Christmas morning." He scowled suddenly. "What's the trouble? Anything wrong?"

"Of course not," Sarah said. "Why?"

"You don't look very happy."

"All right, I'm not," Sarah said. "Sam, I think it's time to tell Kevin about Tully."

Sam eyed her thoughtfully, then fumbled the pack of cigarettes from his shirt pocket, took one out and lit it.

"Don't you?" Sarah insisted.

"Me?" Sam asked. "I've got no thoughts on the subject."

"That means you don't."

"All right, that's what it means," Sam agreed.

"But he has to know sometime, doesn't he?"

"I'm not even sure of that."

"You mean we just forget what we know about Tully writing those letters? We forget what we know about how he financed this?"

Sam exhaled a lung full of smoke, eyed his cigarette judiciously, then looked up at Sarah. "Yes, that's just what we do."

"I hate people who cut corners!" Sarah said, almost passionately. "I hate wise guys and sharpers and chiselers and angles—especially I hate angles, and Tully's playing one!"

"Okay, okay," Sam agreed mildly.

"Okay, what?"

"So you hate 'em."

"I hate them enough so I think they ought to be exposed. After all, Kevin was our first friend, wasn't he?"

Sam only nodded.

"Then why shouldn't we protect him?"

"We should," Sam agreed.

"Then why shouldn't I tell him about Tully?"

Sam turned his head, stared thoughtfully out the window, then he sighed heavily and straightened up. "Maybe the kid's working something out for himself, Sarah. How do you know?"

"No, he's just got that kind of a mind—shifty, evasive and always on the lookout for number one."

"You don't like him, you mean?"

"Damn it, that's just what I *don't* mean!" Sarah said miserably. "I like him. I just think it's my duty to tell Kevin about all of it."

"That's a horrible word, duty," Sam said. "It's got more people in trouble than you could ever count. It makes tattle-tales out of little boys. It keeps men married to old bags they should have deserted years ago and it keeps women mothering drunks."

Sarah was silent a long moment. "What are you trying to tell me, Sam?"

"I'm trying to tell you to keep that cute little nose out of other people's business," Sam said flatly. "All right, so Tully's a nice, dishonest guy. Still he's going to make Kevin a buck along with the one he makes for himself. Why do you care? You going to marry him?"

"No," Sarah said angrily.

"You figure you've got a mission in life to fumigate other people?"

Sarah didn't answer, only stared at Sam with anger in her eyes. Suddenly Sam smiled. "Let it lay, kid, let it lay."

Sarah picked up her purse, gave Sam a long level look and said, "I think you're a bastard, Sam, but I'll let it lay." Outside in the gray day, Sarah still felt her face hot with anger at memory of Sam's words. *Are you going to marry him?* Sam had asked. That was just the point, Sarah thought. She wasn't, so why should she tolerate his dishonesty more than anyone else's?

Nevertheless, when she climbed the stairs to her apartment, she knew she was not going to tell Kevin right away.

Tully could barely see the lights of the Galena station for the driving snow. Some time while he was in the photographer's dark room waiting for the prints to be finished the storm had begun, and he wondered if they were getting the same thing in Azurite and at camp.

He stepped into the chilly station which held nothing in its gloomy waiting room but a cold stove and a shivering dog. He bought his ticket and went out the opposite door onto the platform alongside which the mixed train was drawn up. Tramping down the platform past the single box-car to the lone passenger car, he was about to swing up the steps when the brakeman descended. It was the same brake-man who'd been on duty when Tully first hit Azurite, and he recognized Tully.

"Hi, Lieutenant."

"Just plain mister," Tully said, grinning.

"How you like that icebox up there in Azurite?"

"I haven't got the full treatment yet," Tully replied. They chatted a moment, both of them stamping their feet against the cold. The still damp photostats in the pocket of Tully's down jacket were comforting to him as he felt them against his glove.

Presently the engine bell began to clang and the brake-man, with immemorial custom, slipped a watch from his sweater pocket, consulted it, then signaled the engineer, say-ing, "Better climb up."

When Tully tramped into the sparsely filled car, a couple of enormous women, shapeless in their winter coats, were blocking the aisle, so Tully took the first seat available to him and stared out at the station which slowly drifted be-hind him as the train began to move.

The brakeman came on through the car, letting a cold drift of air blast in as he exited. Tully stared moodily out into the night, his thoughts on the day's happenings. It had been the wildest kind of luck that Beth had turned up what she had at the Mahaffey. Yet, if it hadn't been for Sarah and her knowledge of county affairs, they might still be wonder-ing who the Gold Medal Live Stock Association was, even if they were curious enough to care. It was really Sarah's do-ings.

Scowling now into the night, Tully remembered how Sarah had put her hand in his when Beth had announced her failure at the bank. Had this been simply an offering of sympathy just as her weeping on his shoulder had been a demand for sympathy? He didn't know, but he wished he could say he didn't care. The trouble was, he cared deeply.

Someone passed up the aisle past him and entered the

washroom, and still Tully stared out into the night. By next week the Sarah Moffit would be operating again, but before that happened he must do something. He must, he knew, tell Kevin of the letters. He had lived with knowledge of that guilt long enough to be wearied to his very soul. So far Kevin hadn't been harmed by anything Tully had done. Luck had enabled him to make it possible for Kevin to mine his claims. Now was the time to lay the cards on the table, and to throw himself on Kevin's mercy. *Why should he have any?* Tully thought gloomily.

He heard the washroom door open. Out of the boredom of inactivity, he turned his head incuriously to regard his fellow passenger.

He was looking at Ben Hodes.

At sight of Tully, Hodes halted abruptly, a blank surprise in his heavy face. He was wearing the dark overcoat, black homburg and dark blue suit of a prosperous traveler to the city.

For a bewildered moment Tully tried to account for Hodes's presence here. It occurred to him then that Ben hadn't driven his car to the mining meeting and that the new snows on the high passes had put a caution in him. A kind of elation tightened his chest as he said dryly, "Hi, neighbor."

Ben scowled. "You been to the convention, too?"

Tully laughed. "Nothing that dull, Ben. Sit down and I'll tell you where I've been."

A deep suspicion came to Ben's dark eyes. His big body sank gingerly to the musty seat as he regarded Tully in silence.

Tully remembered the photostat in his pocket, and then he thought, *Why not here? Why not now?* Reaching in his pocket, he drew out the manila envelope, took out one of the photostats of the Gold Medal Live Stock Association Trade Name affidavit and wordlessly handed it to Hodes.

Ben studied the photostat. Slowly, then, the blood surged in his face, and when he looked up there was plain murder in his eyes.

"Beth?" he asked.

"Partly," Tully conceded. "Partly Sarah, partly me, but mostly that noble forehead of ivory under your hat."

With a savage motion, Ben balled up the photostat and rammed it in his pocket.

"Want another?" Tully said. "I have a dozen."

Ben could only glare at him, and now Tully leaned forward. "Unbutton your coat and relax," he invited. "We're going to have some conversation. Right now, I'll do the talking."

"I bet," Hodes said bitterly.

"Tomorrow morning," Tully began, "you're going to call up Wishnack and Byers and tell them what I want. First, I want the county cat to clear away that roadblock. Then I want the cat rented to me. Mine will be repaired in a week, but I can use two." He halted. "Who was it that shot at me, Ben? Who smashed the fuel pump? Who sugared the compressor tank?"

Hodes only shook his head in refusal to answer.

"Whoever it was, Ben, you'd better call them off tonight."

Hodes did not even signify he'd heard.

"Another thing. I want an easement through the Jote Smith Claim, Hodes. I want it recorded tomorrow morning."

He paused, and still Hodes said nothing, only watched him with a bottomless hatred.

"When I get the road finished," Tully continued, "I'll want to rent a four-wheel drive from the county. I'll also want the county to maintain that road during the heavy snows or else pay my crew to maintain it with my rented equipment. I'm saving the best for the last, Ben."

Tully paused, a faint smile on his lean face. "I'll be obliged for a ninety-day extension on my note. I'm sure you'll be happy to fix me up. Also, you're in the custom milling business now. You're going to mill my ore at the Mahaffey."

Hodes's voice, when he finally spoke, was thick with anger. "If I don't?"

"A grand jury gets the photostat."

Hodes sighed shudderingly. It was pure reflex, as if his animal energy must have some outlet. He had never taken his glance from Tully, and now he said, "My friend, all this may happen, but for you it will happen from a hospital bed."

Tully felt a wry amusement. Ben was predictable; his ultimate recourse was always to violence. "You never learn, do you?" he jibed. Ben rose, and without another word walked back down the car.

Now Tully relaxed against the seat. He could see no way that Ben could retaliate so long as the photostats were safe. The photostats weren't even necessary, he reflected; the records at the Galena courthouse were always available.

The brakeman came into the car and halted beside Tully's seat. He called back into the car, "You ready, ladies?"

Tully looked over the back of the seat and saw the two big women tying bandannas around their heads. To the brakeman he said, "What's up?"

"We're letting these two ladies off at the schoolhouse crossing. Shorter trip home for them."

"Pretty rough night," Tully observed.

"Oh, they're always met," the brakeman said. "If they ain't, we take them on in to the Pine Creek station."

The train began to slow now, and the two women waddled down the aisle and past Tully. Behind them came Hodes. He had taken off his overcoat and suit coat, and now he turned to Tully.

"I think it better be now, Junior."

Tully frowned and slowly came to his feet. "In here?" He looked about him. "It's a little crowded, and the railroad company might have something to say about it. Maybe the passengers, too."

"Turning chicken?" Hodes asked levelly.

"Why, I'd do anything for you, my friend," Tully said. He was shucking out of his down jacket as Ben said, "Come along, then."

Before Tully could ask where, Hodes opened the door and

stepped out onto the platform. Tully followed him down the steps where the brakeman, lantern lighted, was standing in the snow talking to the husbands of the two women. A car's headlight lit up the night with its twin snow-slashed beams. Ben stepped to the ground and with his heavy voice, interrupted the conversation.

"Hoagy, you in a hurry?" Ben asked the brakeman.

The brakeman looked blankly at him, not knowing what to answer.

Ben reached into his pocket and pulled out a bill. It was a fifty, Tully saw. "Split that with the crew," Ben said. "Just keep this packet here until we're finished."

The brakeman pocketed the bill, and asked, "Doing what?"

"You'll see." Ben looked up at Tully who was standing on the middle step. "You coming?"

"Where? Out for a snowball fight?"

"Come along," Ben said heavily. He turned and tramped along the boxcar toward the engine, as Tully, bewildered, stepped down into the driving snow. *He's crazy,* Tully thought, but a pride just as grim as Hodes's, if not as ridiculous, pushed him into motion and he followed.

The bewildered ranchers and their wives watched uncomprehendingly. Tully heard the brakeman mutter something inaudible to them, and then he was aware that the whole group was following him.

Ben reached and passed the engine cab under the serene gaze of the engineer, and then halted beyond the cowcatcher. The engine's headlight lit up a vast world of swirling white. Ben lifted his arm now and pointed to a level stretch ahead along the right of way. "What about there?"

"You're an impatient man," Tully observed. "What the hell, are you crazy?"

"I just don't like to wait," Hodes said levelly. "It'll either be there or right here."

"Lead off," Tully said.

Hodes tramped out into the driving storm to the level spot. Tully followed, and he in turn was followed by the two enormous women, both their husbands, the brakeman, the engineer and the fireman. No one spoke a word.

Ben, his shirt already plastered wet against his massive chest, halted. The moment Tully halted Ben came at him. It took Tully only five seconds to learn that he'd better get his back to the engine headlight. Something he did not see in that blinding glare caught him in the chest and knocked him flat.

He rolled quickly in the wet snow, came to his feet and, fists at his side, circled to his right. Ben charged again, and Tully nimbly skipped farther to his right. He was conscious of the silent group ringed around them, and for one brief second was aware of the wild absurdity of this. Then he saw Ben wheel, halt and squint against the glare of the headlight.

Tully wasted no time. He came at Ben with merciless speed; with every ounce of his weight behind his left arm, he drove his fist high into Ben's solar plexus. With the butt of his right palm, he drove his hand into Ben's shelving jaw, lifting. The two blows were almost simultaneous. Tully heard Ben's great sigh as the wind was driven from his chest. Ben stepped back, fighting the need to bend over, and now Tully, his back still to the headlamp, swarmed at him. He drove at Ben's midriff unmercifully. But this time unlike the other, he wanted to mark him. Time and again he slashed at Ben's face, always keeping his back to the engine, and he was driven by an impatient swelling fury.

Ben first tried to set himself, and then tried desperately to wrestle Tully around so that Tully faced the light. But time and again Tully chopped at his arms and then at his face. He could see the blood gushing from Ben's nose, staining his once-white shirt and even the trampled snow.

Now Ben covered his face with his arms, and suddenly lunged straight at Tully in a diving tackle. Tully brought his knee up to Ben's face, but Hodes's momentum carried him on. Tully felt those massive arms wrap around his thigh and he felt himself lifted.

He landed with a bone-crushing jar on the frozen ground.

The fall had broken Ben's grasp, and now again Tully raised his knee into Ben's face. He heard Ben's groan, found one leg free and kicked savagely at Ben's head. Ben rolled away, cursing wildly, but Tully was quicker. He came up in a crouch and dove at Ben, landing across Hodes's body and driving it into the snow. With an animal ferocity now, Tully straddled him, and with a savage heave turned him on his back. Relentlessly then, his knuckles bleeding, his fist bones electric with pain, he drove blow after wild blow at Ben's head. His arms seemed leaden, so heavy they were difficult to lift.

He felt Ben's body bucking under him, and with a blind and stubborn ferocity, he hit harder.

Ben's body suddenly stilled, and then Tully was aware that someone was holding his arms. He fought furiously to free himself, but could not. He was dragged to his feet, and held erect as he drew in great gusts of the cold, wet air.

Head hanging, leaning against the brakeman and engineer, he spent a full minute fighting for breath. When he had it, he raised his head and looked at the man on his right.

It was Hoagy, and he said, "That guy bought himself a package."

Tully swiveled his head to look down at Ben, who was lying utterly still. One of the ranchers was bent over him, his bare hand placed on Ben's bloody shirt over his heart.

"Well, you never killed him," the rancher said cheerfully.

Tully pushed away from the brakeman and the engineer, turned and stumbled back toward the train. He heard Hoagy say to the engineer, "Well, he bought a ticket, so I guess we load him."

Tully was first off the train at Azurite, and he did not wait to see how the train crew would handle Hodes. His hands were throbbing in spite of the soaking he had given them in the tepid water in the washroom, and he was enormously weary. He tramped down past the panting engine to skirt it, heading for Kevin's in the eight inches of new snow.

Here in the high mountain valley, sheltered from the

wind, the snow was falling straight and soundlessly. More than once as he felt his way across vacant lots, he stumbled over objects covered by the new snow.

Once in the river bottom, he saw Kevin's lights were still on. He was glad, but in any case he would have waked Kevin, since the deep urgency to shed his guilt was in him. Skirting the rotting boardwalk, he knocked on the door, then turned impatiently to regard the silent night.

When the door opened, he turned and for a moment, seeing Sarah standing there, he remained silent.

"Oh, you're back," Sarah said, and smiled, opening the door wider. "Everything go all right?"

Tully stepped inside, a sudden pessimism within him. For a fleeting moment he resented Sarah's presence, and then he thought, *She's got to hear it too sometime.*

"Just peachy," Tully said, and freed a grin.

Old Kevin appeared in the kitchen doorway, and Tully said, "Hi, old-timer." He heard Sarah's footsteps approaching, and turned to her.

"Tully, what happened to your face?"

"Ben was on the train. We got a few things settled—like county help on the road, like an extension on my note at the bank, like renting more equipment, like using his mill."

"You fought with him." It was a statement more than a question, and Tully carefully watched the concern in Sarah's eyes.

"I did," he said. Slowly then he drew his gloved hands from his pockets and unzippered his jacket. He knew that his broken hands and bloodstained shirt would be an unpleasant sight, and he also knew that if he exposed them he would be diverted from what he had come to do.

Kevin said, "Come out in the kitchen, boy. Take off your things."

"I'm still cold," Tully said, hoping this excuse to keep on his jacket would seem natural. He waited for Sarah to pass ahead of him, and then he followed her into the kitchen. She and Kevin had been drinking coffee, and now Sarah, as

Tully sank into one of the chairs, took down another cup and poured him some coffee from the big pot on the stove. Old Kevin settled himself gently into a chair, and smiled at Tully.

"Busy day, son, wasn't it? It's coming almost too fast for me." Tully kept his gloved hands in his lap, and he was aware that Sarah, at the stove, was watching him alertly, as if sensing something was amiss.

Tully took a deep breath, and then plunged. "It's not over yet, Mr. Russel," Tully began. "I guess it's time I mixed some of the bad with the good. I'm sorry it has to be this way."

Kevin frowned. "What way is that?"

"I'm a crook, Mr. Russel," Tully said flatly, his voice low and stubborn. "You see, I didn't like your son Jimmy. In fact, I hated his guts. Twice I sat on promotions for him." Tully paused, watching Kevin to see what effect his words would have on the old man. Kevin's expression was one only of kindly patience; Tully's words seemed to have held no surprise for him.

Tully continued, "Still, no matter what kind of trash you think a man is, you talk with him—especially if you're both hurt, captured and lying fifty miles behind enemy lines. I already knew some of Jimmy's background. It was while we were prisoners that he told me about the Vicksburg Claims. I also knew that Jimmy was going to die. They were paying no attention to his gangrene."

Again Tully paused, knowing how cruel his words were and how necessary. Sarah, while Tully was talking, had come over to stand beside Kevin. She was watching Tully with an expression that in this serious moment he could not fathom. She seemed almost pleased by his ugly words.

"When we got to the San Diego Hospital," Tully went on, "I had set my mind on a fast buck. I got to thinking I'd fought enough of the other guys' war while he was making dough. I knew I'd be out as soon as I was well. But to what? A company job that maybe I wasn't well enough to hold down?" Tully shook his head. "That didn't seem very smart when, with a little luck, I could make a play for the big kill. By that time Jimmy was too far gone to stop me even if he'd known what I was going to do. Do you know what that was, Mr. Russel?"

"I do," Kevin said softly.

Tully looked at him blankly. "You do?"

Kevin nodded. "You were going to write me pretending you were a stranger writing for Jimmy. You were going to say what a wonderful man Lieutenant Tully Gibbs was. You were going to say it so often in those letters from Jimmy that I'd believe it. You hoped to get a share in the Vicksburg Claims."

For fifteen long seconds Tully was speechless, and then he said, "How did you know I wrote those letters?"

Old Kevin smiled gently. "Why, to begin with, what those letters of Jimmy's said just didn't sound like him. He was a mean boy, and all his life I never heard him say a good word about anyone. That got me suspicious. So when you showed up, I went to the hotel and asked Earl to let me see your registration card." Old Kevin lifted his fragile shoulders in a shrug. "It was the same handwriting as the handwriting in those letters. You wrote them all, praising yourself. I figured if a man thought he was that good, he ought to be allowed to prove it. I figured as long as you were on the level with me, I'd keep quiet. You were—and I did."

Tully nodded once, and said bleakly, "Well, now you know." He grimaced. "I'm country rock, Mr. Russel—no showing worth a damn." And he raised his glance to Sarah.

Without speaking, Sarah skirted the table, bent over and kissed him on the mouth.

In total bewilderment Tully looked from her to Kevin, who was smiling.

"I'd suggest," old Kevin said, "that you carry on from here, son."

Tully knew then that old Kevin Russel, shrewd, patient and forgiving, had gambled on him, hoping his ambition, his greed and his stupid dishonesty would burn out of him with time.

Tully felt his throat tighten with emotion, and he looked up into Sarah's face, his glance questioning.

Sarah said, "You heard the man. The same goes for me."